STORM OVER UTOPIA

After the Second World War, Britain looks forward to a brave new future. The University of Central UK creates an experimental model of society: a push-button environment of ease, with an artificial brain at its heart. Located on a remote Scottish isle, it starts off with great hopes. Then snags arise. The great electronic brain begins to malfunction in an alarming manner, and the ideal society is thrown into turmoil . . .

Books by A. A. Glynn
in the Linford Mystery Library:

CASE OF THE DIXIE GHOSTS
MYSTERY IN MOON LANE
THE SYMBOL SEEKERS
GUN FEUD

A. A. GLYNN

STORM OVER UTOPIA

Complete and Unabridged

LINFORD
Leicester

First published in Great Britain

First Linford Edition
published 2016

A catalogue record for this book is available
from the British Library.

ISBN 978–1–4448–2806–1

Published by
F. A. Thorpe (Publishing)
Anstey, Leicestershire

Set by Words & Graphics Ltd.
Anstey, Leicestershire
Printed and bound in Great Britain by
T. J. International Ltd., Padstow, Cornwall

This book is printed on acid-free paper

1

Troubles on the Island

Dwelling in New Society was like dwelling in Utopia, thought Ted Clemence, as he strolled along the ribbon of pavement running alongside the settlement's main road with its central line of electronic studs. These were but one of the wonders making New Society unique among centres of human population. They were connected to 'Auntie' — a creation which, in this year of 1948, was known as an 'electronic brain' — and they meant that cars, electronically linked to them, were actually driven by Auntie. A driver had nothing to do except sit back, and now and again adjust the steering slightly. All the stress and strain of driving was eliminated.

So many stresses and strains of other aspects of everyday living were also eliminated by Auntie's myriad connections throughout the settlement. She took care of a dozen household chores in the comfortable bungalows which housed New Society's staff, so winning the deepest gratitude of the unmarried members and bringing to the wives of the married men the very last word in labour-saving devices. Everything from the drudgery in the offices concerned with monitoring the effects of life controlled by a man-made brain, to guarding the colony through the cordon of electronic security sensors placed alongside the stout wire perimeter fence, went back to Auntie through her countless connections.

This balmy spring evening brought elation to the heart of Ted Clemence. He had a feeling that life was beginning to be good to him. In his background were six years of wartime service as an RAF pilot which had immediately followed his graduation in sociology and anthropology from the University of Central UK. He could still hardly believe his good luck in receiving a letter from his old university soon after demobilisation. It offered him a post on his old faculty with the opportunity of participating in important new studies to do with shaping post-war society. So here he was in this miniature self-contained wonderland, built by the university and covering a considerable acreage of Benarbor, an isolated island off the north-west coast of Scotland.

On the island there toiled a collection of enthusiastic academics, scientists, and ancillary workers and their families, living life under the benevolent care of Auntie. There were high hopes that such a life would become the norm of urban living in the centuries yet to unfold. Each specialist, according to his or her field, checked and counter-checked the daily performance of Auntie in keeping New Society's lifeblood flowing.

Ted Clemence, a heftily-built athletic bachelor, was charged with reporting on the sociology of the settlement, which had been functioning for only three months. He would note how it settled down as an entity in which there was more leisure than in the outside world. So far, there was an unruffled quiet all round, with a general appreciation of New Society as a novel concept. But Clemence knew that, as in any human society, tensions would inevitably develop. There would be factions, disagreements and maybe dangerous feuds. Possibly, tiny New Society might even go the way of whole nations, and disintegrate in revolution and chaos.

On the other hand, though so many in the outside world considered the whole experiment to be a ludicrous adventure whose cost might have funded projects they felt more worthy, it might turn out to be the perfect pattern for life in the brave post-war world. Possibly, every civilised society would eventually follow its blueprint, busily ticking over on a course of labour-saving and easy leisure; each with its equivalent of Auntie, the electronic wonder, as pacemaker.

Clemence glanced towards the white domed building which housed Auntie, sitting on its hill against a clear island sky. He nodded to the construction and muttered: 'Old lady, I just hope you can safely deliver all the bright promises we expect of you.'

At that moment, he saw a lone blue car approaching on the road. He recognised it as the vehicle of a good friend: Paul Lindley, an electronics engineer. As it approached him, he saw Lindley relaxing behind the wheel, grinning at him and allowing Auntie to attend to the driving. The car passed him with a double toot of its horn; then, almost as soon as he turned his head, Clemence heard the harsh *swoosh* of tyres on concrete. He swerved around quickly to see that Lindley's vehicle was off the road and on the pavement, with its bonnet hardly inches away from one of the stout lamp standards.

Clemence began to run the short distance to it, thinking that some emergency had caused Lindley to override Auntie's control and apply the brakes, as was possible if some crisis called for it. He arrived at the car just as Lindley opened the door and started to climb out. He was ashen-faced.

'Are you all right?' panted Clemence.

'Yes. I'm okay. Can't imagine what happened, though,' said Lindley with a panicky edge to his voice. 'Everything was going quite normally with Auntie in control, when the car suddenly swung over, mounted the paving and headed straight for this lamp post. I managed to grab the emergency brake just in time. Phew, talk about a close shave! It looks as if Auntie decided to play another little trick.' He leaned against the car, panting and took out his handkerchief to mop his brow.

'What do you mean? Has she tried something like this before?'

'Yes, she gave Jean, my wife, a terrible scare only yesterday. You know the little domestic robots we have in the houses, running about on wheels and doing so many household chores?'

Clemence nodded. 'The servos? Of course I know them. Everyone in New Society has one including me.'

'Well, we call ours Fido, as if he's a pet dog. He's very handy and quite trust-worthy — at least, he was until yesterday. Jean used him to bath the baby, young Buster. With his multiple arms and light touch he's quite capable of giving the baby a good bath and towelling him down. In fact, Buster is tickled pink by him.

6

Yesterday, Jean left Fido to do his stuff in the bathroom while she was busy in a bedroom. Suddenly, Buster was yelling the house down!

'She rushed into the bathroom and found the baby dumped on the floor in a pool of water. Fido was standing in a corner, totally immobile. He has no face, of course, he's only a collection of versatile arms controlled by Auntie, but Jean swears he was smirking at her in triumph.

'Buster was safe enough. He's hardly a year old but he's a tough little bruiser. I felt Auntie could hardly have started her own personal revolution . . . but this affair with the car makes me wonder. Can it be that she has it in only for me and my family? I've never heard of anyone else having such trouble.'

'Oh, I wouldn't think in those terms, Paul. I can't imagine Auntie is really in revolt. I'm sure your two instances are just the result of some temporary kink in her workings, and by sheer coincidence you, Jean and the baby were involved,' Clemence said. 'Still, if it looks as if Auntie is developing antisocial habits, we should talk to Dr Archnov, the Director, about it.'

'Maybe we should,' agreed Lindley. 'I'll think about it when I get my breath — and my nerve — back after this little escapade.'

'The car seems to be all right. Luckily, we can drive our cars independently of Auntie, and I suggest you do that,' said Clemence. 'Or, since you're a bit shaken up, would you like me to drive you home?'

'No, no, I'm quite all right,' Lindley assured him. 'But I'd like to know if these events mean that Auntie is turning nasty on us.'

'I'm sure she isn't,' said Clemence dismissively. 'This whole set-up is pretty vast and wholly new. If we must blame Auntie, let's put it down to early growing pains.'

'Maybe, but it's no joke when you think she can put you within a whisker of severe injury — or even death,' said Lindley, climbing into his car.

'Well, have a safe journey home, and give my regards to Jean and your young bruiser,' Clemence said.

He watched Lindley back the car on to the roadway then drive it homeward. He turned and looked at Auntie's white dome on the far hill. The housing of the gigantic electronic brain was a bland, modernistic structure reflecting the bright sunshine.

'Are you as quiet and peaceful as you look, Auntie?' he said aloud. 'Or are you hatching some dire plot?'

2

Visiting Dignitary

The beginning of what promised to be a warm and sunny spring was making itself felt in London's Gower Street. That elegant thoroughfare of houses that were stylish creations in the earlier years of the nineteenth century, many of which were still the homes of notable personalities, was rising to the occasion. In the invigorating sunshine, people of business bustled along; students from University College at one end of the street carried their books; art students from the neighbouring Slade School of Fine Art, all displaying studied attempts to look like raffish bohemians, humped their big folios of work; and, now and again, cars passed, most of them looking rather new. The wartime restrictions on automobile construction and petrol consumption had recently been relaxed, although the general level of household income did not run to a high level of car ownership.

Standing at the window of the upper room of his house, Hereward Hynes looked down on the street scene with a slight smile. There seemed to be an infectious vigour about the passing show. The rigours of early 1948 and the shuddering recollection of its snowy February had passed away. Now, with the chill dispelled from everyone's bones, there was a vibrant spirit of new beginnings in the air.

The large car that came purring along from the Euston Road end of Gower Street was certainly not new. It was sleek and gleaming and looked as though it had been created for the world of the rich, probably in the nineteen-twenties. Furthermore, it bore the stamp of wealth, being chauffeur-driven.

'Great heavens, it's stopping here,' muttered Hynes. Surprised, he watched the vehicle halt at the kerb outside his premises. A uniformed driver, a rarity in that era of austerity, stepped out on to the pavement, opened the rear door and stood beside it with the stiffness of a military man. A heavily-built man, slightly stooped and no longer young, emerged. He wore a costly-looking overcoat and a grey trilby hat.

'A toff if ever I saw one,' announced Hynes to the empty room. 'I'd best look brisk and busy, and see what Miss Budd brings up the stairs.'

He moved quickly towards the large desk placed almost in the centre of the room. It was an antique which had been part of the room for almost a century; like the desk, the room itself held the trappings and air of late-Victorian opulence. This house had been owned by Hynes' grandfather, and then his father. As a young man, his grandfather had known all the notables of Gower Street, including the painters and poets of the Pre-Raphaelite Brotherhood who used to gather a few doors away.

The room was still in tune with the sumptuous days of Victoria's reign. It had a crystal chandelier while brocaded chairs stood along the walls. There was a large and comfortable leather armchair in front of Hynes' desk for the ease of his clients.

Hynes was a private detective, a tall, lean and fit man. In a weak moment, he might just admit that he was nearing middle age and that a little touch of grey was showing at his temples but he still looked the sprightly Grenadier Guards officer who had, in the recent war, fought his way through some spectacular adventures.

Down at the street door, the elderly visitor mounted the half-dozen steps and yanked the old-style bell-pull. The door was opened by a short and plump woman in a black costume. She had horn-rimmed spectacles and her auburn hair was cut into a severe pageboy style. The term 'redhead' carried implications of a reckless and feisty spirit, which seemed misplaced in middle-aged Miss Tilly Budd — but when one noticed the occasional twinkle in the eyes behind her glasses, one might know she was not entirely a mechanical servant of strict business.

The newcomer touched the brim of his hat to her.

13

'Good morning, madam,' he said. 'I've called on Mr Hynes, though I have not made an appointment. The name's Artingstall.'

'Good morning,' nodded Miss Budd. 'Do step inside, Mr Artingstall.'

'*Sir* Elkanah Artingstall,' corrected the elderly man and Miss Budd noticed a distinct north country burr in his voice.

'Forgive me, Sir Elkanah,' she said. After closing the door, she operated the inter-office communication set standing on a small table in the hall. 'Sir Elkanah Artingstall is here to see you, Mr Hynes,' she said into the mouthpiece, in a grave and businesslike way.

'Show him up, please, Miss Budd,' Hynes replied from his desk, while his brain posed the question: *Who the devil is Sir Elkanah Artingstall?*

'Straight up the stairs and through the door immediately at the top, Sir Elkanah,' directed Miss Budd, indicating the wide stairway. 'May I take your hat?'

Artingstall handed her his hat and mounted the stairs.

At the very moment he was opening

the door to admit the knight, Hynes remembered something of Artingstall's fame. It had to do with cotton. Elkanah Artingstall was noted for his string of mills in Lancashire, all now working full pelt to meet the demands of the post-war export drive. He had been lauded by the press as embodying the spirit of the poster declaring: *'Britain's bread hangs by Lancashire's thread.'*

Hereward Hynes shook the visitor's hand and waved him towards the deep armchair by the desk. He noted that Artingstall's face indicated he had not had an easy life, but still it hinted at a good-natured disposition. He was reputed to be a millionaire several times over but nothing about him suggested luxurious living.

'Would you care for a drink, Sir Elkanah?' Hynes asked, moving towards his desk.

'Nothing alcoholic. Tea's good enough for me, Mr Hynes,' stated the knight gruffly as he seated himself in the armchair. 'I started as a poor boy, you know. Grew up in a mill town among working folk. They were the very salt of the earth, but drink

15

was a curse in those days, and I saw many a good man ruin himself and his family through it. I'll have none of it. I believe in putting money to better use.'

'I'll have my secretary, Miss Budd, bring us some tea,' Hynes said, flipping the switch of the inter-office communicator. 'Now, how can I help you, Sir Elkanah?' he asked after ordering tea.

'They say you're about the last of the old crew who were established around Baker Street. I mean fellows like Kenton Steele and Clive Markham, Jack Keen and Colwyn Dane and that chap with the monocle, Falcon Swift, and the lean one who had a big bloodhound and an assistant who was a mere boy. The papers were full of their exploits before the war.'

'You put me in distinguished company. I can only do my best in the same line of country,' said Hynes.

'Don't be so modest, Hynes,' grunted Artingstall. 'I know the reputation you've built up in the short time since the war. I know there are plenty who'd come to you with a problem before they'd go to the police.'

'And your problem, Sir Elkanah?'

'Ever hear of cybernetics, Hynes?' asked Artingstall briskly.

'The science of building man-made electronic brains? Yes, but I know next to nothing about the subject,' admitted Hynes.

'Well, I'm Chancellor of the University of Central UK. Not that I'm an academic, but I advised the university on organising some courses of business studies, and was surprised when they put me up for election as Chancellor. I'm a lifelong bachelor and have no family whatsoever, but I've always believed in giving younger generations a chance. I became increasingly interested in the work of the university and the notion occurred to me that, with the world of learning entering a phase of post-war expansion, I'm wealthy enough to fund a worthwhile project.

'I heard of an interesting and novel scheme suggested as a collaboration between the university's Department of Sociology and its newly created Department of Electronic Engineering. It's headed by a brilliant chap, Professor Archnov, a Ukrainian. I understand he went through a rough time in the war. He was pretty much a penniless refugee at the end of it, but he's back on his feet and has settled in this country.'

As Artingstall was speaking, elements of a lengthy magazine article he'd read some time before were awakened in Hynes' memory. He recalled the name of Archnov, and that he was connected with the subject of the article — a highly unusual social experiment promoted by Artingstall's university.

'Isn't Professor Archnov the man guiding that experimental society on a Scottish island, where everything is controlled by a giant man-made electronic brain?' he asked.

'Exactly. It's his brain-child in a technological sense, but I funded almost the whole of the project. It could be the blueprint for a brave new world now that the war is behind us. I can see that the world is changing. The industries such as mine — based on establishments like noisy, grubby and labour-intensive mills — will quickly pass away. It struck me that ventures such as the one the university was embarking on could be the basis of a society where humanity might flourish without need of irksome labour — a near-perfect leisure culture. I saw such a society as a fine gift for future generations. After all, I witnessed my widowed mother almost permanently exhausted through scrubbing floors day in and day out to feed me and my brothers and sisters in those bad old days.' There was a quiver of emotion in the knight's voice.

'And am I to understand that there is something about the venture calling for the services of a criminal investigator, which is why you are here?' asked Hynes.

There was a pause as the ever-dutiful Miss Budd brought in tea and biscuits. After her departure, Artingstall took a sip of tea; then leaned forward in a confidential way, saying:

'I'm not sure how much of a criminal matter it is, Hynes, but I've been receiving disturbing mail concerning the experiment on the isle of Benarbor. Both the island and the New Society experiment are pretty much self-contained and closed communities. The island is owned by the university. It was totally uninhabited and was bequeathed by a benefactor long ago hopefully for use in the likes of natural history studies of climactic affairs.

'Then the war came, and the RAF and Army established a base for coastal defence there. There's a small airstrip, left over from those days. It is now used by a private aviation company to fly in supplies and newcomers to New Society from the mainland. There are a few old military huts used by New Society, but the bulk of the buildings and roadways were created for the project by the university.

'The only inhabitants are Professor Archnov and his staff of scientists, academics, technicians and their families, plus a few labouring and ancillary workers. They're generally considered to be a happy family, living in their quiet backwater and keen as mustard on the work in hand.'

Artingstall paused, produced his wallet, and said: 'I'd like you to look these over.' From the wallet, he took two scraps of paper and laid them on Hynes' desk.

They were rather grubby and tattered and the paper was lined, seeming to have been torn from some cheap notebook. Artingstall indicated one, saying: 'This was the first to arrive in my mail, about eight days ago, and it was followed by the second one yesterday.'

The handwriting on the first of the notes was scrawled in pencil and was clumsy, as if the work of someone unused to penmanship. Also, Hynes noted peculiarities about the formation of the letters.

He read: '*So, you rose from poverty to prosperity but chose to give your money to a project of wickedness devised by a twisted mind to debase the human spirit and creative energy. Nothing but the most horrifying evil can result from such a course of action. When it all fails and bitter failure stalks the ruins it will be far too late for you to regret the folly of your undertaking!*'

Hynes read the note once, then a second time, examining every line, rubbing his chin thoughtfully. He turned to the second missive, obviously written by the same hand, giving it equally careful scrutiny. He read:

'*The shiny promise of the wonder world of the future cannot cancel out the fact that you are actively furthering the murderous villainy of the past. You funded a twisted notion of human progress. You may be sure severe retribution will fall on you!*'

'Have you any idea who sent these notes?' asked Hynes. 'Have you encountered any sort of opposition to what the university is doing on Benarbor?'

'Nothing really concrete,' said Artingstall. 'I haven't been to the island or anywhere on the nearby mainland. I'm growing old, you know. I have little taste for travel these days but I take a great interest in how my funds are being spent and I'm in constant touch with Professor Archnov and some of his senior staff. They don't know of any serious opposition to the New Society experiment, but some people recalled rumours among the mainland population claiming the work on the island is merely a cover for something sinister.

'The ridiculous belief is that the real

22

business is concerned with atomic bombs, so there's a likelihood of things going wrong and the island plus a great lump of Scotland being blown to bits.'

Hereward Hynes smiled. 'That's to be expected from rustic greybeards. Ever since Hiroshima and Nagasaki, the world has feared atomic bombs. There's certainly a threatening note to your communications, and a disturbing mention of death, even if nobody is directly threatened. There's even a hint of religious fanaticism. Are you the only one to receive such notes?'

'Yes, I'm the only person to be targeted,' said the knight.

'No doubt that's because the popular press publicised your funding of the New Society,' said Hynes. 'Maybe some harmless crank has a bee in his bonnet about the work on the island and these notes contain nothing but empty bluster.'

Artingstall fumbled in a pocket and produced two crumpled envelopes which he laid on the desk. 'The notes came in these. You'll see from the postmarks that whoever bears ill will towards the university — or to me — is living close by.

They were posted in Fort Calaige, the nearest point on the mainland to Benarbor.'

Hynes gave him a tolerant smile. 'Correction, Sir Elkanah. The postmarks merely prove they were posted in Fort Calaige. Whoever posted them might live far away from there.'

'Wherever he lives, I can't get over the feeling that he means business, and that these notes have come from someone who is more than a mere crank, Hynes,' declared Sir Elkanah firmly. 'It's just something about which I have a very strong hunch. All through my business life I had hunches about good moves or bad ones, and they rarely played me false.

'I believe something dangerous is brewing up there in the Western Isles, and I want to engage you to go up there and investigate — and nip it in the bud.'

Hynes looked dubious. 'I'm not sure the whole thing isn't just a matter of some eccentric who goes in for writing crackpot letters, Sir Elkanah,' he said. Then he noticed a shaft of bright sunlight streaming through the window and saw the smiling blue skies of spring over the rooftops across the street. As if dispelled by the burgeoning magic of the season, the lethargy of the long winter fell away from him, and the notion of a sojourn in the rugged far Western Isles had an irresistible appeal. Besides, he wanted to know more about the novel experiment in progress on the isle of Benarbor. He added decisively: 'Nevertheless, you can consider me engaged.'

'Good,' said the knight. 'I've had a few ideas aimed at making things easier for you, which I'll put to the university authorities, so you can have free access to the island and move about New Society unhindered. Since the life and career of Hereward Hynes are so well known to the public, I suppose you will want to take on an assumed identity — that can be arranged. Allow me to brief you on the university and its role in New Society, and on the setup on Benarbor and in its locality.'

Artingstall and Hynes put their heads together. For another quarter of an hour they were in deep and detailed conversation. Then Sir Elkanah took his leave and

Hynes escorted him down to the street door. The detective then stepped into Tilly Budd's downstairs office.

'I shall be leaving London in a few days, Miss Budd, so I'll have to ask you to mind the shop,' he announced.

Miss Budd looked up from her desk with an expression suggesting she was somewhat affronted. 'Indeed!' she said. Her air of severe professionalism was dropped when she was in private conversation with Hynes. On those occasions, whatever she had to say was firmly stated and came straight from the shoulder.

'I hope, Mr Hynes, that when you ask me to mind the shop you do not expect me to take on your far too active role as an investigator,' she sniffed. 'I have seen your confrontation of criminality cause you to return home with black eyes, a split lip, a bandaged head and, on one occasion, a broken arm. I also know that, several times, you have dodged bullets. I most emphatically refuse to indulge in that side of the business.'

Hynes looked at her with a whimsical expression. 'Come now, is this the Miss

Budd who was a warrant officer in that noble gathering of female soldiers, the Auxiliary Territorial Service, speaking?' he said. 'Are you telling me that you never enjoyed a bar-room brawl or two in your soldiering days?'

Tilly Budd tossed her head haughtily. 'You know very well that the ATS never went in for that sort of thing,' she responded. 'I shall undertake the secretarial duties I am hired to provide and nothing more.'

Hereward Hynes adopted the guise of a man put emphatically in his place, but the sharp-witted Miss Budd did not miss the playful twinkle in his eyes. 'My dear, invaluable Miss Budd,' he intoned, 'I only meant that you should keep the diary up-to-date and make a careful record of any phone calls coming in, while I'm away for an unspecified spell.'

'An unspecified spell? I hope you are not off to some dangerous place at the ends of the earth, Mr Hynes,' responded Miss Budd more softly, allowing a chink in her armour to give a glimpse of the affection she felt for the detective.

'No, only to the Western Isles in Scotland.'

'Hmm, it all sounds very peaceful. I do hope it turns out that way for you, Mr Hynes,' said his secretary.

On the ground floor of the spacious house was the valuable library which both Hynes' father and grandfather had collected; and which, along with the house and a considerable fortune, was bequeathed to Hynes. There he spent some time poring over a large atlas which contained detailed maps of the British Isles. He studied a chart of Benarbor which, at the time of publication, was labelled as uninhabited. It was a long sliver of land with some sparse forestry indicated at one end and an irregular-shaped lake at the other. The map-maker had grandly styled this a 'loch', though Benarbor was far too small to accommodate a genuine loch on the grand Scottish scale, and this water was little more than a relatively modest pond

There was a straggle of low hills along one side of the island. Hynes had learned from Sir Elkanah that New Society now took up most of Benarbor, and that the wartime airstrip was not far from the loch — but, like New Society itself, was not marked because the map predated the war.

Even as he stared at the map, Hynes wondered if he was wise in taking up Artingstall's engagement — or was he merely giving in to a springtime itch to leave London for the lure of the sea and wide open skies of the Western Isles?

After all, there was no suggestion of real criminality in such evidence as the knight had placed before him. The scrappy notes sent by post made mention of some kind of destruction to come, but they might be only the lurid ramblings of a crank. On the other hand, they might indicate an intention to harm the project which the knight was backing financially.

He did not know that, only the day before Sir Elkanah called on him, there had occurred the incident of Paul Lindley's car running loose from Auntie's electronic guidance; while the day before that, Lindley's household robot had turned rebel when bathing the baby. Nor did Sir Elkanah Artingstall know of those events, for word of them had not left the island.

Furthermore, Hynes was not to know that, during the evening of this bright spring day, something quite remarkable and sinister would be enacted on Benarbor.

3

Intruder From the Sea

A cool evening breeze stirred the shrubbery along the margin of the 'loch' on the isle of Benarbor, and the sky was darkening over the Atlantic, forming a vast panoramic background to the island. The loch stood some distance from the New Society settlement; which, in the fading daylight, seemed to be a village whose clutter of buildings showed scattered electric lights. On its fringe, some of the outer buildings associated with the functioning of Auntie, all now without lights, straggled along toward the loch.

In addition to the shrubbery around the loch, there was a stand of trees, stunted in growth because their lives had been spent in battle with the Atlantic gales. In the trees there stood an abandoned Nissen hut, a forgotten relic from the wartime days when military forces occupied the island. Weeds choked the environs of the structure and rust was attacking the corrugated metal of which it was created. A few windows remained, blackened and cracked, but others were gone. In a healthier condition, such a hut would have a door at either end. Now, one remained, but the other was missing.

There was a stirring in the shrubbery. Any observer familiar with New Society would be startled to see that, moving along, finding its way over rough ground — and, by some magical instinct, following vague pathways through the shrubs — was a servo. It was one of the household robots used by the population of New Society, of the kind that had startled Paul Lindley's wife by rebelling and dumping her baby on the floor.

This servo made its appearance out of a clutter of overgrown shrubbery crowded around the base of a low, isolated structure that was part of Auntie's electronic system, connected to the 'brain' on the hill by a multitude of cables laid over the ground. The servo was a simple but ingenious creation whose main feature was the set of versatile arms ending in multi-fingered hands that could grasp all manner of implements or tools to accomplish a variety of chores. It travelled on an arrangement of wheels set in a housing which permitted them to mount steps, and which were remarkably high-powered. They could ride over any minor obstacle they encountered, such as straggling roots or portions of fallen branches and rocks which might be on the ground among the clumps of shrubbery through which the servo travelled. But servos were not meant to function outdoors in rough country. Their role was to perform in the homes of New Society's residents in obedience to the electronic power of Auntie, sitting in serene dignity on her far hill.

Showing itself to be even more startlingly rebellious than 'Fido', the one which had misbehaved itself when bathing the Lindleys' baby son, the servo drove persistently onward through the shrubbery. It wheeled across a weed-invaded and broken surfaced pathway, and entered the yawning opening bereft of a door at the end of the Nissen hut.

Thirty minutes later, as the skies had darkened further, presaging dusk, the servo emerged from the hut and slithered through the shrubbery on wheels that seemed to be stronger than before. Indeed, had there been any witness to observe its behaviour, the device would have shown itself to have an overall increased alertness.

The Lindleys had given their servo the name of a pet dog, 'Fido'; and, though it had no face or any feature to liken it to a flesh-and-blood creature, this servo in the overgrown forgotten end of the island seemed now to have acquired a very distinct and almost dog-like personality. It moved through the shrubs much like a hound confidently treading a path he knew well by instinct. It headed directly for the set of shrubs near the low building from whence it had emerged.

The fictitious witness, had he been able to scrutinise the hands of the servo, would have seen that there were now more of them — and, if he had sufficient technical knowledge, he might grasp the point that, since its visit to the decrepit Nissen hut, the servo could accomplish more tasks than before. Furthermore, it would seem to accomplish them in a way suggesting it knew what it was doing.

Nearly an hour passed. The dusk gathered, the screeching seabirds winged high in the vast Atlantic sky, and the salty wind rustling the vegetation on the fringe of the loch was edged by the chill of evening. The solitary door of the Nissen hut creaked open and a man slipped out of it. He was slender, no longer young, with the lean, deeply-lined face of one who had endured bitter hardship. He moved quickly with his body bent low as if trying to make himself into just another evening shadow. He skirted the loch, melted into the stunted trees beyond the water, and scrambled down a rocky incline which brought him to the edge of the ocean.

There, he negotiated rocks that stood along the fringe of the water, lapped by the waves. Between two of them, beached, was a light boat, powered by an outboard motor, with its stern presented to the open sea. The man expended some energy in hauling the craft about and shoving it over the rocks and into the sea. He pushed it until it was fully afloat and he was knee-deep in the water, then he climbed aboard and set off with the engine put-putting on a low note. He steered the boat towards a low grey line on the horizon, dotted here and there with pinpoints of light. It was the mainland directly opposite the straggling form of the isle of Benarbor.

In rapidly encroaching darkness, the man smiled as he thought of how slickly he had breached the security of New Society, the alien entity planted on Benarbor. For, although the social experiment was guarded by an elaborate and forbidding fence high enough to defeat attempts to climb it, and the fence in turn was guarded by its series of electronic sensors, these measures did not totally isolate the settlement. Only three sides of New Society were covered by them. The designers saw no point in fencing off the fourth side where the university's site straggled away towards the loch, the old remnants of the military installation and the open sea. The notion of entrance being made on the seaward side was totally discounted.

The man in the boat grinned and shook his head as if despairing of those great brains in faraway England. Something momentous had already started in New Society, and he had just taken steps to bring about developments even more so.

⋆　⋆　⋆

In faraway England, the following morning was hardly in its stride when Hereward Hynes was disturbed at his extra-early breakfast by the ringing telephone. Later that morning he was to take the train for Scotland to undertake his investigations at Benarbor, and now he found himself listening to an excited Sir Elkanah Artingstall, blurting out a message as rapidly as he could speak.

'You'll never believe it, Hynes!' he spluttered. 'I felt all along there was trouble brewing on Benarbor, and now it has happened. In fact, it started a couple of days ago, but Professor Archnov and his people didn't tell me at first. It has to do with the technicalities of New Society, and Archnov and his scientists wanted to trace the origins of the problem before telling me about it. Indeed, although he agreed to the cover story I concocted to account for your presence on the island when I called him on leaving you, he held back on the new problem facing New Society, He hoped he and his staff would soon solve it. But it has defeated them. They're totally baffled and Archnov called me soon after dawn to tell me about it. Of course, he knows you are leaving for Benarbor today, and he and his staff are anxious to meet you.'

'And what is the problem, Sir Elkanah?' Hynes prompted.

Sir Elkanah Artingstall hardly paused for breath in rapidly relating the story of what looked like the revolt of New Society's great guiding spirit, the electronic brain, Auntie. He told of the servo's treatment of the Lindleys' baby and the unprecedented action of Paul

Lindley's car in running free from Auntie's guidance, bringing Lindley close to injury or death.

'Have any more instances followed those two?' inquired Hynes.

'No, but it seems all New Society is alarmed. There's a general feeling that Auntie is biding her time and possibly plotting to spring some unpleasant surprise. There is great unease. Archnov is worried that, if their families are threatened, some of his key staff will pack up and leave the island, and the whole project will be ruined. The bulk of these people have only just settled down. All are valuable, and if they become disillusioned and leave, it will be disastrous.'

'What do you think is at the root of Auntie's behaviour — some form of sabotage?' asked Hynes.

'Perhaps. Archnov is reluctant to think something of that kind has occurred, and he and his specialists have not so far found any evidence of specific acts of sabotage in the mechanism. The only other answer is that Auntie had fits of craziness. In other words, the man-made brain is subject to mental illness — but Archnov dismisses that idea,' said the knight. 'This affair appears to give some point to those messages I received.'

'And since New Society is a small and isolated community, suspicion of sabotage suggests an inside job, perpetrated by someone within that tiny community,' mused Hynes.

'Exactly. The situation is very serious.' The elderly man at the other end of the telephone sounded more agitated. Doubtless, he feared that his treasured hopes for the pioneering blueprint of a revolutionary leisure society, so much in tune with the post-war spirit of renewal, were about to be dashed.

'You can't get to Benarbor a minute too early to tackle this business, Hynes,' he urged.

'I am on the very point of leaving to take the train from Euston, Sir Elkanah,' Hynes assured him. 'I am going by rail rather than driving. The long journey will give me a chance to think over the procedure we discussed when you were here, and how I should act on it.'

Within an hour, Hynes was steaming out of Euston on the first leg of a journey which would take him to Glasgow. Thereafter, following an overnight stay in that city, there would be more tedious travel by rural routes to the north-west coast of Scotland; and, at Fort Calaige, he would become a passenger of the small airline that would take him to Benarbor's airstrip. He knew this first portion of his trip would be the most comfortable one and he settled into his well-upholstered seat, thinking of the mission before him.

From his wallet he took out the missives received by Artingstall and the envelopes in which they were sent. He had requested that the knight let him keep them and Sir Elkanah had agreed, only too willing to give Hynes a free hand in tackling the mysterious affair on Benarbor. From the start, the style of lettering of those scrappily-pencilled notes had interested Hynes, and now he wanted to take a closer analytical look at them.

A couple of minutes of staring at the letters brought him to a realisation of what was characteristic about them

41

— they were formed in a way marking them as Continental. A Frenchman might have written them, or perhaps a German — or, for that matter, someone from any one of a swathe of European countries. Though the language was quite grammatical English, it might be inferred that the notes were not written by an British person.

He examined the envelopes which were addressed to Sir Elkanah Artingstall's town house in London. There was a figure seven in the address and, most tellingly, the numeral was written with a bar crossing the downward stroke.

Hynes pursed his lips and nodded confirmation of his first suspicion. The Germans, the French and nationals of an unknown number of countries throughout Europe put a bar across the downstroke of the numeral seven, but never a British person. It was not taught in British schools where youngsters first gained knowledge of writing, elements of which would last a lifetime.

This suggestion of the notes having a European connection caused Hynes to wonder if a definite start to his investigation might be made by pinpointing someone of distinct Continental background; possibly in Fort Calaige, from where the notes were mailed, or somewhere in the vicinity of the town. Or perhaps even on the isle of Benarbor.

He did not know what the situation in Scotland was but, since the war, more populous parts of Britain had received a great number of Continental immigrants. There were refugees galore from many countries who had settled in the country, as well as various Allied ex-servicemen who had decided to settle down in Britain. Many were men who had married British girls during the war. There were also former enemy prisoners of war who had no desire to return home. Additionally, he knew of a recent influx of men and women known as EVWs — European Volunteer Workers — who had been uprooted from German-occupied countries as slave labourers; and who, after being held in refugee camps, could not return home. Their countries were now under unwelcome Soviet control which had replaced their pre-war national governments. Britain, needing to rebuild extensively after the war, eagerly welcomed these additions to the work force.

Scotland, of course, being smaller and less industrialised, must have absorbed fewer of the post-war floating alien population, one of whom might have written the notes. On the other hand, Hereward Hynes, never one to readily accept anything at face value, argued with himself that the notes might not have a Continental hand behind them, but were possibly the work of some knowledgeable person familiar with Continental written style and who employed it as a smoke-screen.

Though his acquaintance with New Society was still only sketchy, the sole person of European background involved in the project he had heard of was the chief of the venture, Professor Archnov; a Ukrainian who, as Artingstall had stated, had endured a disrupted time during the war. But it was highly unlikely that the scientist, now back on his feet and making a far-reaching contribution to his field of endeavour, would send rather woolly threats of some disaster to pester the man who financed what must surely be the dream project of the scientist's career.

Before receiving that morning's phone call from Sir Elkanah, Hynes felt that the knight might be making too much of what could be merely the ramblings of some eccentric, perhaps a nature-lover who feared the scientific venture was despoiling an attractive island. Then word of the danger-ous events suggesting that Auntie was losing her grip dispelled his notion that his jour-ney to Scotland might prove a wild goose chase.

There was clearly something wrong on Benarbor — but could what began with a robotic device ill-treating a baby and a driver being sent dangerously off-course end in the 'horrifying evil' and 'retribu-tion' so luridly forecast in the notes?

He smiled ironically, thinking of Sir Elkanah's visit to him before news of the ominous happenings on the island reached him. The knight had already thought out a role the detective might take as a cover, and described it:

'I would never tell you how to conduct your business, Hynes, but I feel you should be incognito on Benarbor,' Artingstall had said. 'You are well known as a criminal investigator and you've made plenty of headlines. It might spread further alarm if all New Society knows a private investigator has been engaged, not to mention alerting some saboteur in the ranks. I suggest you pose as a journalist who is contemplating writing a book on New Society.'

Then, in his phone conversation on the morning of Hynes' departure, when he had news of Auntie's disturbing behaviour, Artingstall displayed an energetic eagerness to be involved, even at a distance, in what might turn out to be an adventure on the island.

With almost youthful enthusiasm, he revealed that he had devised a form of script for the detective's role on Benarbor.

'I've been thinking over the matter of your posing as a journalist, Hynes,' he said. 'I suggest you call yourself Edgar Herford to keep your real name and your true purpose dark, just in case someone within the New Society experiment is secretly opposed to it and has engineered Auntie's revolt. Of course, I must tell Professor Archnov who you really are, and pledge him to entrust that knowledge to only his closest aides. Is that all right with you?'

'Of course,' Hynes said.

'You might even be moved to produce a real book to make your disguise more convincing,' suggested Artingstall, almost puckishly. 'A book giving a positive picture of the New Society experiment, of course. I'll ring the professor and inform him that everything is arranged. He and his staff will be ready to receive you and arrange accommodation for you.'

The train carrying the man who now called himself Edgar Herford chugged ahead, with the scenery beyond its windows changing from the orderly vistas of the Home Counties and the midlands to the increasingly rugged landscapes of the north and the borders. At various stations, those sharing Hynes' compartment came and went: businessmen, families, youthful National Service conscripts in the army and RAF who had scarcely started shaving. It was borne on Hynes that they all represented a familiar world he understood, while he was headed for the challenges of a totally artificial society, smitten by what appeared to be a mysterious malady.

Word of the advance of that malady reached him at the end of the initial stretch of his journey. From the small Glasgow hotel where he was to spend the night he telephoned Artingstall to inform him that he had arrived in Scotland. At the other end of the phone, the knight's voice was grave. He no longer sounded like a schoolboy anticipating an adventure.

'It's a good thing you've arrived, Hynes. I got word from the professor of more trouble in New Society just today. It seems another chap was attacked by one of those robot contraptions. I haven't got all the details yet, but it seems it injured him. You'll probably learn much more when you reach the island tomorrow,' he stated.

Hynes frowned. He wondered if Auntie was laying on a welcome for him.

4

A New Arrival

Ted Clemence learned at first hand of Auntie's newest aberration. The previous evening, Clemence was strolling through the housing colony of New Society, having left his flat a short time before. He was heading for the colony's social club, intending to enjoy an evening beer and some conversation with whoever was gathered within its hospitable walls. The comfortable club, with its mixture of men and women from every level of the experimental society, was useful for obtaining a view of current trends in its daily life, and Clemence's brief was to monitor New Society's development as a social entity.

He was alone on the stretch of pavement between the houses until he reached a bend in the footway and became aware of a figure coming towards him, progressing slowly with a limp. As the man neared him, he recognised white-haired Dick Smythe, an elderly long-serving administrative officer of the University of Central UK. He and his wife had spent decades in devoted service to the smooth running of the institution. Both were now close to retirement age. Clemence, in the early planning conferences to create New Society, suggested that older generations should not be excluded from the experiment because, if the project truly proved a blueprint for a new future, senior generations and their welfare would have to be accommodated. Smythe and his wife, Beth, eagerly volunteered to sample life in the island community for the rest of their working careers, and pronounce upon its impact on citizens who were no longer young.

Concerned by Smythe's obvious mishap, Clemence drew closer and called: 'Why the limp, Dick?'

Smythe looked disgruntled. 'Twisted my ankle, and you'll never guess how. I was dodging my servo at home. It was standing idle in a corner, then it suddenly seemed to take a dislike to me. It wasn't even switched on, but it somehow started itself and came at me with its arms flailing, obviously meaning to hit me. I was sitting down, reading, and I jumped up quickly, then stumbled just as the servo was inches from me. Luckily, Beth was in the room — you know how the servos are plugged into the domestic power supply? Well, Beth quickly grabbed the flex and yanked it out of the socket. The trouble was, I twisted my ankle in my hurry to get out of the way. I've just been to the dispensary and Dr Willis strapped it up. I managed to walk. I wasn't going to risk driving after that scare with Paul Lindley's car, and my experience seems to have been almost a repeat performance of the business with the Lindleys' baby.'

'Can I give you a helping hand to get home?' offered Clemence.

'No, thanks. It's only another few yards.'

Nevertheless, Clemence took his elbow to ease the pressure on his injured joint, walking him the short distance to his front door.

'Does Professor Archnov know about

the servo?' he asked.

'I haven't told him yet, but I'll ring him now I'm home,' answered Smythe. 'Dr Willis said he'll call him as well. He doesn't want to spend all his time doctoring victims of wild servos. It makes me wonder if this business isn't getting out of hand, in spite of the professor saying all will very quickly be put right.'

Clemence nodded. He was thinking of how Professor Archnov had called a meeting of all New Society's residents in the big social hall, and reported on Paul Lindley's near-miss with his car and the incident with the Lindleys' child. He assured everyone that, while these events could not be immediately accounted for, the cause and a solution would soon be found. All the while, however, Archnov appeared to be conscious that his assurances lacked conviction, and his voice seemed to be edged with panic. The idea of Auntie staging a revolt was becoming common currency, and no doubt Professor Archnov had frightening visions of his carefully-nurtured dream collapsing in chaos.

Clemence strode onward deep in thought. As a sociologist, his business was human behaviour. He had expected that, in one form or another, there would be inevitable problems in New Society. None of the imported inhabitants were natural dwellers on a small, tranquil island, and some disruption might result from yearnings for large cities and bright lights.

Some might come to feel that New Society — for all its vaunted boasts of shaping the future — was, in fact, limited and stifling. Ultimately it could prevent some, particularly those who had fought in the war, from enjoying the benefits of the longed-for peace they hoped would reign in the wider world. He thought of myriad obstacles that might plague marriages. A wife could hanker after the bright sophistication of shops where the newest fashions could be found; a husband might simply desire wider horizons, the bonhomie of pubs and the vigour and noise of sporting occasions.

Clemence was not naïve. His training caused him to envision dozens of reasons why New Society's environment might cause discontent, and perhaps even outright revolt, among human beings. What he had never reckoned on was a man-made mechanism such as Auntie undergoing a form of mental aberration and reacting against its creators. After all, Auntie was not a brain at all. She was a thing of electronic impulses, synapses, and currents of energy speeding through a baffling complexity of circuits. She had no business taking on the sensitive vulnerability of that remarkable creation — the human brain.

* * *

The following day, slow railway journeying along minor branch lines brought Hereward Hynes through landscapes of heather and small cottages beside neatly laid-out crofts. It was mid-afternoon when he humped his baggage across an isolated concrete apron close to the township of Fort Calaige.

Squat hangers and outbuildings stood beyond the strip against a wide, cloudless sky, and the salty tang of the nearby sea was in the air. This was the headquarters of Fort Airways, a small airline set up by a group of young aviation enthusiasts who, only a few years before, had been stalwarts of the Royal Air Force.

On the concrete apron stood a single aircraft: a compact, short-bodied plane which looked nimble and highly manoeuvrable. An athletic, sandy-haired young man in grey dungarees came striding over the concrete with a hand outstretched in greeting.

'Welcome. You'll be Mr Herford,' he said in the lilting accent of a Western Islander. 'I'm Alec McLeith, one of the directors of Fort Airways. I'm to fly you over to Benarbor. We're just getting on our feet here — started up when we were demobbed. Only one aircraft as yet, but we have great hopes of growing.'

Hynes shook his hand and nodded towards the plane. 'I see it's a Westland Lysander,' he commented. 'A sound little workhorse.'

Alec McLeith grinned. 'Ah, you know the Lysander? Are you ex-RAF?'

'No, Army. But I had some experience of Lysanders.'

'She's a bonny wee bus. I was in heavy bombers myself, so you can understand how handling that wee beauty is as easy as riding a bike,' chuckled McLeith. From this first meeting, Hynes liked this open-faced young man with the unmistakable hearty cheerfulness peculiar to former RAF aircrew.

Hynes saw no reason to elaborate on his acquaintance with the Westland Lysander, dating from his secondment from the Guards to a secret department headquartered close to London's Baker Street, that thoroughfare so closely associated with criminal investigators and undercover activities. In 1948, this department was still wrapped around by the Official Secrets Act, and the general public knew next to nothing of it. Its function was to train a motley selection of agents from various nations under enemy occupation, and facilitate their distribution around the occupied territories for purposes of espionage and sabotage, as well as to arrange their return to England when necessary — if they lived to accomplish their missions.

In the case of Occupied France, agents

were frequently dropped by parachute, while others might be delivered on the coast in darkness by a speedy little felucca, a boat adopted from the Middle East. Frequently, the sturdy Westland Lysander was used to fly agents in to secret landing fields organised by Resistance groups. Likewise, they could be returned to England through the hazardous means of being secretly collected by a Lysander. A good portion of Hereward Hynes' military secondment had to do with riskily accompanying agents and equipment on flights in and out of France, which was held in the tight grip of the Nazis and their collaborators.

'If you know the Lysander, Mr Herford, you'll know there's room enough for yourself and your luggage in the rear compartment,' said Alec McLeith. 'Come along and we'll make a start.'

He picked up one of the detective's bags and the pair walked towards the plane.

'I can't class the landing strip on Benarbor among the great airports of the world, but it's adequate,' he said. 'Some

57

of the workers on the university project have been trained in airport fire and safety routines, as required by law, so our landings and take-offs are properly supervised. That's something Professor Archnov arranged from the start. A canny man, is the professor. He doesn't leave loose ends.'

Soon, to the well-tuned song of the Lysander's engines, Hynes and McLeith were winging across the sea. The briefest of flying-times brought them over Banarbor and Hynes looked down in wonder at the layout of New Society, spread out below: a vital structure of neatly-designed living quarters and buildings connected to both the functions of Auntie and the university administration.

And there was Auntie, sitting, content in the sun, above this whole throbbing manifestation of human activity. Here and there, human beings were in evidence — some walking, a couple of men chatting on a corner, a young woman pushing a baby carriage — and there were a few cars, travelling alongside the lines of highway studs, doubtless under the control of Auntie.

Previously, Hynes had seen Benarbor simply as a sketch map on the page of an old book, but now he saw its modern layout — how the creation of New Society had changed it into what seemed to be an orderly and well-regulated social entity.

He noted the high fence circling the settlement on three sides and he saw how, at the extreme fourth end of the site, facing the ocean, there was no fence. The enclosure was simply left to peter out in the tangles of rock on the fringe of the Atlantic, as if they provided sufficient secure coverage.

He tried to force his memory to retain this eye-in-the sky image of the whole of the island and New Society as an aid to future reference.

Below them, quite close to the body of water grandly styled a 'loch', a ribbon of concrete came into view. It was the old wartime airstrip and was not in the best state of repair. Half a dozen overall-clad men began to run across it and take up positions, ready to supervise a landing.

The Lysander came in smoothly, losing height and touching down easily with only an occasional jolt as its landing gear rode over cracks in the runway.

'Everything all right, Alec?' called one of the ground staff, running alongside the slowing machine.

'Aye, all running sweet as a nut,' answered McLeith. 'I've brought Mr Herford in.'

'Good. Professor Archnov and some of the chiefs are waiting yonder.'

The aircraft halted and, in its rear compartment, Hynes gathered his baggage and made ready to descend by the fixed ladder running down to the ground.

He had noted that ladder with interest. It indicated that this aircraft had seen wartime service of the kind all too familiar to him. Such ladders were an afterthought, added to the Lysanders used for penetrating the Nazi 'Fortress of Europe'. Under dangerous conditions, when speed was imperative, they helped to hasten agents when leaving the aircraft or embarking on it. Hynes wondered if he had encountered this very Lysander during those fraught secret operations.

On the edge of the landing strip stood five men whose overcoats and raincoats flapped in the sea breeze while they held down their trilby hats. To give them a newly-coined title, these were 'boffins', the elite among scientific toilers. Their appearance suggested academics transplanted from the quiet confines of the world of learning to this rugged location of waves, rocks and salty winds.

Chief among them was a tall man in late middle age who carried a briefcase. He had a ramrod-straight back and moved forward with efficient briskness to shake hands with Hynes. He wore thick-rimmed glasses and, nearly central in his forehead, was a dark, almost square, strawberry birthmark.

'Mr Edgar Herford. Come to research your book on our efforts here,' he said in a soft but heavily-accented voice. 'You are most welcome. I'm Feodor Archnov and these are my closest colleagues, all prepared to give you any help you need.' He indicated each man individually: 'Professor Jones, Professor Estcourt, Dr

Glassman and Dr Thorne, all highly specialised and invaluable to our university's departments of electronics and electrical engineering.'

There was more handshaking and Hynes noted each man's characteristics. Jones was bearded; Estcourt had a clipped military moustache; Thorne was chubby, with a bland, clean-shaven face. Only Dr Glassman came near the popular idea of the contemplative and slightly detached professor. His moustache was straggling and somewhat unkempt while wisps of grey, unruly hair escaped from under his trilby.

Professor Archnov unexpectedly breached his stiff and proper demeanour by treating Hynes to a large wink. In a stage whisper, he said: 'Of course, Mr Herford, these gentlemen know who you really are, but they are the only ones who do and they will keep it strictly secret.'

In a normal voice, he added: 'Come, my dear sir. It's good to have you here. We will take you to your accommodation. We need to walk a little way into the housing section. Then I suggest that you and I, with these gentlemen, meet in my office to familiarise you with the situation in New Society.'

The housing section was a neatly-laid-out arrangement of buildings, mostly prefabricated but of pleasant and comfortable appearance. Some were homes suited to married workers on the project, and others were long bungalow structures housing flats for those who were single. Hynes felt that any sense of remoteness was eased by a snatch of radio music drifting from one of the houses. It filled the air with the rather languid cadences of Russ Morgan's song *So Tired*, a number that was all the rage in the world beyond Benarbor that spring.

The accommodation assigned to Hynes proved to be a compact and comfortable three-roomed apartment in one of the bungalows sectioned into flats. It was situated in a corridor lined with the doors of what were plainly similar dwellings. As he opened the door for Hynes, Archnov nodded to the next entrance.

'Your next-door neighbour is Ted Clemence, a tutor in anthropology and sociology. His function here is to study New Society as a societal entity,' he said. 'He knows what makes it tick, and you might find him useful. He, of course, has no idea that you are a private detective.'

With the four academics in tow, Archnov showed Hynes around the premises. It was fitted with everything Hynes needed, plus the futuristic refinements which only New Society could boast.

Hynes was quickly instructed in the use of the various buttons on a panel close to the main entrance to the apartment, which controlled a range of labour-saving devices. Hynes nodded to a curiously designed-machine standing idly in a corner. It was mounted on a wheeled base and seemed to be merely a set of arms emanating from a central column.

'One of those offending servos, I take it, Professor,' he observed.

'Yes, it'll handle odd jobs for you. At least, it should if all goes well. I'm pinning all my hopes on the recent troubles with servos being only a passing problem, frightful inconvenience though they are.

I've no doubt we'll soon put them right.'

'And the case of the car that slipped loose from Auntie's control?'

Archnov's face clouded. 'Again, I hope that was also just a temporary aberration. We've not yet traced these incidents back to any technical fault, but I'm sure we shall.' It was plain that the professor was troubled and was straining to make light of his problems.

'If it should turn out that some human agency is behind our difficulties, we all hope your expertise will root it out.'

Hynes nodded, his face as grave as those of his intellectual companions. Inwardly, however, he was experiencing a surge of queries about what was afoot here on Benarbor.

On the surface, it looked as if the problems caused by two rogue servos and the erratic behaviour of Lindley's car could be put down to some massive fault in the great brain called Auntie. So probing into it must logically be the province of electronic engineers and not a criminal investigator.

Then he recalled the strange notes

received by Sir Elkanah Artingstall, which might indicate either harmless fantasies or genuine ill-will towards the benefactor who had financed the social experiment. Was this spirit of ill-will active within the university's personnel on the island? Was it somehow powering Auntie's rebellious behaviour? Now that he was on the ground where the mishaps took place, Hynes saw signs of apprehension weighing on the chiefs of the university establishment.

Archnov's companions were taciturn and silent, as if brooding on the prospect of their pet dream project unravelling before their eyes. Anxiety could be detected in Archnov also. In his case, his optimistic attitude that all would eventually be well and his rather ridiculous hearty surface did not cloak the signs of strain.

Hynes realised that, on the brink of launching himself into the role of a writer researching New Society to cover his genuine purpose, he really lacked a starting point for his investigations. But already he had detected a certain tension shared by Archnov and his close companions which was hard to categorise. He felt a judicious study of the group would be rewarding.

5

Eyeing the Boffin

After familiarising Hynes with the modern wonders of his new accommodation, Archnov suggested a walk to his office, which would give Hynes an opportunity to learn more of the settlement's geography and what it had to offer. As the newcomer and his escort of academics were leaving the front entrance of the accommodation building, a tall, substantially-built man came strolling briskly along the path towards it.

Professor Archnov hailed him with a cheerfulness which Hynes felt was assumed in order to cover his worries about New Society's difficulties. Something about it clashed with Archnov's undoubted alien accent, as if he was striving to play a stage Englishman and not proving very convincing. 'Ah, Clemence, old chap, I just mentioned you to Mr Herford here. He's here to do a book on New Society, as I told everyone over our community radio. We've put him in the empty flat next to yours.' He turned to Hynes. 'Mr Herford, this is Ted Clemence, your neighbour.'

Clemence advanced and he and Hynes shook hands. Hynes took in Clemence's general appearance and put him in his mental file, as he would with many of those he had yet to encounter in this assignment. Clemence's age group and energetic demeanour suggested participation in the recent global hostilities. He was, like Alec McLeith of Fort Airways, of a type familiar to Hynes: one of his own generation, moulded by the hardships of the war. He had the look of one made resourceful and reliable by experience.

'Pleased to meet you, Mr Herford,' said Clemence. 'Since we're next-door neighbours, I look forward to seeing plenty of you. My field is sociology and anthropology. I'm here to study and report back on how a wholly new form of society builds itself up and conducts itself. Not much different from your own activities as a writer, come to think of it. I look forward to chatting to you now and again.'

Hynes nodded and, for the first time, tried to fit into his new persona, which he hoped would become as familiar and comfortable as a well-worn garment. He responded to Clemence jovially.

'It's Edgar, by the way — Ed if you like,' he stated.

Clemence grinned. 'And I'm Ted — Ed and Ted, it sounds as if we should be doing a music-hall act. I'll be seeing you around.' Clemence waved a hand and strode off towards the accommodation block.

The walk to Archnov's office gave the professor an opportunity to point out the various facilities and services set up within the university's domain, which were those likely to be found in a comfortable village. Hynes learned where he might eat and find all the necessities of life.

'We are fortunate in having a set of skilled backup workers and tradespeople who were happy to exchange a life in crowded towns and cities for one in a remote and rather romantic setting such as Benarbor. A good many are vigorous young people who came out of the war eager for something less run-of-the-mill than the existence they endured in the pre-war days,' Archnov said as they reached a section of road lined with small, neat shops.

'Everything to help our people feel at home,' declared Professor Archnov. 'A butcher, a baker, a barber, a ladies' hairdresser and a dress shop. There's a tailor, a green-grocer, and every other service is provided. We have a social club — licensed under Scottish law, of course, through the magistrates on the mainland. Into the bargain, there's a doctor running a dispensary, offering a dental service as well as medical, with a small hospital attached in case any emergencies arise. In fact, we have everything a small town could boast. Of course, our tradespeople give excellent service, aided by the fact that so many of their mundane everyday chores are eased by their equipment being plugged into Auntie. On the whole, Auntie is a pretty good egg — when she behaves herself.'

Like an agent earnestly attempting to sell real estate, Archnov detailed yet more of the benefits of the unique society contained within the electronically guarded high wire fence strung along most of the isle of Benarbor.

'A very agreeable set-up,' commented Hynes. 'And how are your retailers supplied with new stock?'

'A good amount is flown in. We keep Fort Airways fully occupied. Mr McLeith flies his Lysander in regularly and he works wonders, packing a great deal of freight into that little machine. There is also a jetty at the further end of the island where heavier goods and passengers can arrive.'

'And you mentioned the mainland magistrates. What about police?' Hynes asked.

'We have no police presence on the island,' responded Archnov.

'Nor do we need one. We have no desperate criminals and no disorderly drunks,' said a rather sniffy voice from the midst of the academic entourage. It proved to be that of Professor Estcourt, of the clipped military moustache. 'We are, after all, very respectable academics mixed with hand-picked people of the highest moral character.

We have not so far built up a record of crime. We haven't even had any car thefts. We are all a bit above that sort of thing, you know.'

Professor Archnov smiled. 'Professor Estcourt is correct, though he tends to sound rather puritanical. I think it can be taken as read that New Society people are genuinely good eggs, wholly law-abiding. In due course, we'll have quite a model society. We'll have schools when we arrange everything with the mainland education authorities and our youngsters will grow up in a healthy environment run on lines which will be wholly unique — futuristic, in fact. To return to your question about the police, it is agreed that we need only phone the police in Fort Calaige if their presence is ever required, and they'll fly officers here by their own growing helicopter service — or by way of the ever-obliging Fort Airways. And I should point out that, for external security, the outer part of the huge fence surrounding the settlement is guarded by a string of electronic bollards, each connected to the others. If there is ever an attempt to breach the fence from outside, they will set off alarms and mount an unseen electronic wall any bad hats can't break through.'

'Auntie again?' asked Hynes.

'Yes, another useful service from Auntie,' Archnov said. 'The system was devised in our laboratories with a view to eventual use in the wider world as a guard against robbery at banks and other vulnerable places. The whole idea of Auntie-style installations will prove a boon to the future world. On a big scale, the system is complicated, of course. Here and there in New Society you'll see small structures — outstations, we call them — they're something like electricity substations, and keep all the various functions of Auntie running smoothly.'

Hynes nodded thoughtfully. He was beginning to form a picture of New Society as it was seen from the inside by at least some of its inhabitants. He allowed the lessons of such observations as he had made to sink into his brain.

His thoughts were interrupted by Archnov's jovial voice. 'Gentlemen, it is not far off lunchtime. I suggest it would be a good idea to adjourn to my office where we can continue instructing Mr Herford on New Society's affairs while we're tucking into the lunch I've arranged to be prepared by the domestic staff.'

Hynes was again thinking of the professor as an actor attempting the role of a dyed-in-the-wool old representative of the English upper-crust, using terminology such as 'tucking into', 'bad hats' — and, twice, 'good egg'. All jargon which clashed incongruously with his marked foreign accent.

Lunch, served in the privacy of Archnov's well-appointed office in the settlement's administration building, proved excellent: indicating that in a land not yet free of rationing three years after the war, members of the higher echelons of the university's establishment were living quite handsomely. In the middle of the meal, Hynes touched again on the antisocial behaviour of Auntie, the remarkable entity the combined brain power of the cybernetic experts had brought into being.

He asked: 'So far, I'm aware of three instances of Auntie malfunctioning to everyone's alarm: a car slipping out of her control, and two attacks on individuals by servos. Have there been any others since then? And what's causing them — an internal fault in the brain itself, or some kind of outside interference?'

Archnov was quick to answer. 'No, we have had no further difficulties, thank goodness; but three instances are bad enough. I'm sure my colleagues here will agree that the difficulties are undoubtedly caused by internal faults.'

There was a nodding of heads and murmurs of agreement among the academics, but Hynes was thinking that the collective electronic wizardry on the island was taking rather a long time to solve the riddle of Auntie's misbehaviour.

Hynes pushed his questioning in a quiet, conversational way. 'The last of the three attacks was very unusual, wasn't it, Professor? How could a servo set itself working without being switched on?'

Archnov looked decidedly uncomfortable, as if he had hoped this intriguing subject would not be raised.

'That was a rum affair; the servo must have somehow shaken off the central control mechanism of Auntie to go into action.' Looking nervous, as if he knew how hopelessly lame the explanation sounded, he added quickly: 'It's embarrassing to have to admit we may not yet have traced all of Auntie's faults; but our electronic specialists are second to none, and all these gentlemen and I have spent hours at Auntie's very heart, checking and adjusting all her workings.

'I'm sure we're on the way to curing the problems. I can't believe any outside agency is causing them. Consider how insular and tight-knit we are. We are surrounded by our fence, doubly protected by electronic sentinels, and there is no doubt that everyone within the settlement is loyal. We may be sure there are no traitors among us.'

There was more nodding of academic heads and rumbles of agreement.

'And yet Sir Elkanah Artingstall has received letters suggesting there is someone in the outside world, at least — in Fort Calaige, if we believe the postmarks — who is an enemy of New Society,' Hynes pointed out.

Archnov waved a hand dismissively. 'Oh, they could be the work of some crackpot who is probably quite harmless,' he said airily. 'Sir Elkanah is a remarkable man but he is no longer young, and old men grow querulous and are easily frightened. Those messages have probably thrown him into a blue funk, making him imagine there is some frightful bounder lurking in the shadows outside our Utopia, bent on damaging the pet project for which he stumped up a considerable fortune.'

'Yes, the writer is probably some dotty nature lover who feels New Society has destroyed the habitats of the island's wildlife,' put in Dr Thorne, hitherto a silent, rather brooding presence. 'I fear Sir Elkanah takes fright too easily. That's one of the penalties of being well advanced in years.' There was almost a sneer in his voice. Professor Estcourt, with prissily pursed lips, was seen to nod as if approving Thorne's observation.

Hynes maintained a placid face, but behind it, his mind was working overtime. He was picking up interesting pointers to the thoughts of at least some of his companions. Chiefly, there was Archnov: very foreign in his accent but employing elements of argot seemingly absorbed from the schoolboy yarns in the magazines *Magnet* or *Gem*, and making an incongruous figure of himself. Archnov had all but stated the belief that Sir Elkanah's anxieties were those of an ancient teetering on the brink of senility.

There was the taciturn Dr Thorne, who only now had broken his cover of deep brooding to support Archnov's view of Artingstall.

Then there was Professor Estcourt, stiff, seemingly very strait-laced and fastidious. From his earlier observations, he was obviously not in tune with Sir Elkanah's fears.

Professor Jones and Dr Glassman had not revealed enough of themselves to add useful data to Hereward Hynes' mental card-index other than seeming to be deeply thoughtful men, wrapped up in their specialities. He had not yet shaped his observations on all these leading spirits of New Society to claim a firm grasp of the personality of each, but certain interesting indications were beginning to emerge.

He needed no telling that a gathering of high-geared intellects such as were found in a university or large college would have a full measure of opinions, counter-opinions, clashes of theories, outright rivalries, jealousies and bitter feuds. Frequently the calm surface of academe covered dark tides of turmoil.

So far, these leaders of the great sociological experiment had shown him only welcoming good nature at the personal level. However, three — Archnov, Estcourt and Thorne — viewed Auntie's aberrations as resulting from within the electronic brain itself, and which would ultimately be remedied by scientific skills.

So, did it follow that his presence as a criminal investigator was considered a waste of time? And was the feeling unanimous among his hosts?

Hynes accepted another glass of wine when Professor Archnov passed the decanter — it was wine of a higher quality than most being retailed in this economically stringent year of 1948 — then fully tested the waters into which he had been plunged.

'Gentlemen, is there a belief that Auntie's peculiar moods need only some doctoring by your on-site specialists, so there is no mystery and my presence here as an investigator is quite unnecessary?' he asked blandly.

He voiced the words in an almost throwaway manner, then watched their effect on Archnov, Escourt and Thorne, the trio that had just suggested that Sir Elkanah's reaction to the current difficulties was allied to senility. All three now figuratively fell over each other to back away from that suggestion, as if they had been jarred into suddenly remembering that Hynes was in New Society because the university's Chancellor had retained him.

'Absolutely not!' declared Estcourt. 'There *might* be some dangerous outsider, or even someone inside our own camp, a saboteur, up to no good. Sir Elkanah is right to take those warnings seriously.'

'Quite so,' rumbled Thorne. 'Considering the huge cost of our installation here, who can blame him for being cautious?'

Professor Archnov nodded. 'Yes, he

coughed up a thundering great amount of cash to enable our scientific field to take a magnificent leap forward after all the wartime setbacks. Professionally, we owe him a great debt of gratitude. He is right to be concerned.'

And this blatant about-face, thought Hynes, came on the heels of Archnov's slightly scornful observation that Sir Elkanah was alarmed by the notes because his venerable brain power was unravelling.

Jones and Glassman were particularly interesting. Each kept an unmoved facial expression. It seemed neither had an opinion to offer. Hynes recalled the excellence of the meal and the better-than-average wine, and thought that it ill became anyone among this company to denigrate Sir Elkanah. A cynical and ungenerous spirit might conclude that. In this hard-up post-war world, they were living well at the expense of the old industrialist.

This initial contact with the leading lights of New Society gave him food for thought as he settled into his new accommodation for the first night. He laid out his clothing and various belongings, and set up the portable typewriter he had brought with him to add authenticity to the fiction that he was a visiting writer.

He looked around rather cautiously as he prepared for bed, not feeling wholly confident in the reliability of the wondrous devices worked by Auntie which filled the flat.

In particular, he was dubious about the complicated set of arms on a wheeled base, the servo. He unplugged its lengthy cable from the wall socket and told it aloud: 'I'm not taking a chance on being murdered by you as I sleep, my friend.' Then he turned in.

He lay in bed for a spell, thinking over his arrival on Benarbor, his purpose there and the complex personalities into whose company he was thrust. The one who came to dominate his pre-sleep reverie was Archnov, with his slightly ridiculous, transparently more-British-than the-British, pose. Hynes had detected in the professor a constant nervy anxiety. Was this due merely to things going wrong with the huge cybernetic venture of which he had charge? Or was there another reason, something lying behind the façade he presented to the world?

Of one thing he was certain: no matter how stolidly unruffled and calm a front they put up, and no matter how technically expert they were, the New Society boffins had no notion of either what was wrong with Auntie nor how to put it right.

In the jumbled thoughts crowding in on him on the edge of sleep, he recalled Archnov's satisfaction with the strength of the security afforded to New Society by its encircling wire fence and its outer guardians, the string of electronic bollards. But the settlement was not entirely encircled. From Alec McLeith's Lysander, he had spotted the lack of a fourth side to the fence. The end nearest the sea was left open, and blocked only by a tangle of rocks, beyond which lay a stretch of stony beach.

He recalled how, when flying into France to deliver or recover an agent of the secret army from Baker Street, he would scan the inky black terrain with night-glasses, watching for a landmark, or the risky glimmer of a landing fire set by the local Resistance group. He had acquired a quick facility for recognising the meaning or potential of what might be viewed from the air. It was even sharper when exercised in broad daylight.

Sleep claimed him as he thought in a befuddled fashion how much that stony beach at the vulnerable end of the New Society fence resembled ocean-edge locations into which the secret army's feluccas slid to drop or collect agents. How easily an intruder in a light boat might make landfall there, and enter carefully-guarded New Society!

6

Ammunition From Miss Budd

Hynes woke early and, still wary of Auntie's temperamental misdemeanours, avoided the push-button facilities of the flat, apart from using then to supply hot water to ready himself for the day.

His mind was on making a start of establishing himself in the role of author researching a book. He packed a blank notebook and one of the new ballpoint pens — Biros, they were called, from the surname of their Hungarian inventor — into his pocket, not knowing quite how he would proceed during this new day. Uppermost in his mind was the question of whether Auntie had shown any further signs of revolt since the previous night. He decided on breakfasting in the inviting restaurant that had been pointed out to him on his introductory tour of New Society. This would give him a chance to mingle with other settlement dwellers and discover what was in the air.

He was leaving his front door when that of the next flat swung open and Ted Clemence stepped out.

'Ah, the other half of the music hall act!' greeted Clemence brightly. 'Good morning, Ed. What are you doing about breakfast?'

'On my way to the restaurant to get some,' said Hynes.

'Good. So am I. Let's go down together.'

'Glad to. Have you heard if all is still quiet with Auntie?'

'Can't say, but we'll soon hear if there is any news when we meet up with other people over breakfast,' Clemence said.

The spacious restaurant bustled with activity as New Society's inhabitants prepared for their day's duties. Hynes and Clemence took their places in the queue at the long counter, and Hynes saw how Auntie aided the serving staff, slickly delivering generous breakfasts on trays which slid out of various slots in response to push-button orders.

Clemence called to a man ahead of them: 'Is anything happening with Auntie, Jack?'

'It seems not, otherwise, we'd have heard about it. You know how news travels.'

'Hmm — the old lady on the hill is very docile. I hope this is not the quiet before some sort of storm,' murmured Clemence.

He and Hynes found a convenient table in a quiet corner and, as they started breakfast, Hynes said: 'I'm making a start on collecting data for my book. I thought a good beginning would be a pen-portrait of Professor Archnov as the leader of the project. He seems to be a fascinating personality. Can you give me a brief picture of him? Of course, I'll flesh it out with a personal interview with him, when he has time to give me one.'

'What can I tell you about Professor Archnov?' asked Clemence. 'Well, much about him is remarkable. He gathered all of us together when we started off on the New Society venture. He said all involved should know something of the man in charge. He's a Ukrainian, as you know, and mustn't be considered a Russian even though the Ukraine is part of the Soviet Union. He outlined his background, which, as a sociologist, I found fascinating.

'Before the war, he was studying advanced electronics at Kiev University. He'd shown remarkable aptitude in the field when quite young, and the educational authorities in his home region nurtured him and pushed him into further education. The Soviet government was keen on scientific advance above everything else, and young Archnov could do no wrong.

'However, there was something about which the Soviet state knew nothing. Archnov had never been on their side. In fact, he hated the Moscow government and, under the surface, the dutiful student looked for a chance to escape. When he was very young, the Ukraine set up an independent republic but it was swamped by the Soviet Union. Eventually, the Soviet regime cynically engineered an artificial and mercilessly cruel famine in the Ukraine, causing starvation on a vast scale.'

'Ah,' said Hynes. 'I recall news of it reaching the West. As I remember, it was punishment for the Ukranian farmers' refusal to enter the Soviet collective farming programme and lose their independence to state control.'

'Exactly. Archnov was deeply affected by it and never forgot it. When Hitler invaded Russia and the Ukraine in 1941, he got his chance. He joined the Ukranian Insurgent Army which fought both the Germans and the Red Army in the hope of regaining Ukrainian independence. After only a short time, everything from the Insurgent Army's point of view fell apart under the pressure of the Nazi advances in the Ukraine. Archnov's unit was severely beaten and collapsed in chaos. Many members tried to flee the Ukraine.

'When Archnov told us about it, he said he could still hardly believe his good luck. He somehow got to Odessa on the Black Sea, and his luck held. He managed to persuade the skipper of a neutral tramp steamer to take him across to Turkey. All the time, he was keeping some of the newest data on cybernetics from his university days locked in his brain.

'Turkey was still neutral at that time and the Allies hoped it would eventually support them. Turkey was playing a curious double game, supplying raw chemicals to the Germans while Britain had agreed to train pilots of the small Turkish air force. I know about the last bit because I'm ex-RAF aircrew, and I once met Turkish cadets in Britain in the early part of the war.'

Hynes recalled aspects of international affairs in wartime, learned in briefings in Baker Street.

'Turkey was a hot proposition in those days, wasn't it, Ted?' he commented. 'I recall tales of the capital, Ankara, being a hotbed of spies — Allied and Axis — and a very dangerous place.'

'Yes, but Archnov seems to have fallen on his feet there. He didn't go into details, but admitted he was pretty well destitute when someone connected with British espionage discovered him, learned of his background in advanced electronics, and saw his value to the British war effort. Arrangements were made to smuggle him to England, flying him in with a contingent of those very Turkish air cadets. Very soon he was working on British wartime scientific projects.'

Hynes grinned. 'And somehow, in all his adventures, he managed to pick up the vocabulary of the Greyfriars School Remove and the cast of P.G. Wodehouse.'

'Yes. It's rather comic.' Clemence laughed. 'He seems to have been so overjoyed to be in England, and part of the British academic establishment, that he lays on the English character act with a trowel. Still, he's a good man, and he knows the cybernetic field backwards. At the end of the war, a number of universities were vying for his services.'

They concluded breakfast and Clemence said: 'Archnov created something quite remarkable in New Society, but snags are showing up. I'm particularly interested in the effects on the community of apprehension about Auntie's misbehaviour.

'You must have noticed the strain on people. They are wondering if and when

Auntie will spring another surprise, although nobody is panicking or talking too much about it. I'm equating their stoicism with the old wartime spirit of keeping calm and carrying on. But this is a totally novel and untried society. It owes its very existence to its control by Auntie, and there are indications that the control might be failing.

'What will happen if the whole fabric of the brave new Utopia — this blueprint for how the world will live in the future — falls apart? Think of a miniature version of old Russia disintegrating when the Czar's regime collapsed, or Nazi Germany when the Third Reich crumbled under the Allied onslaught. I think you'll see that the prospect would keep any sociologist on his toes and wondering if, in the end, he'll be reporting on a tale of great scientific success or only the collapse of a bright-eyed dream?'

Hynes nodded thoughtfully, then said: 'Yes, I suppose the complete collapse or the total impairment of Auntie would cause the demise of New Society as a working unit.'

'You bet it would. I keep wondering if Auntie's malfunctions result from something other than ordinary technical faults, such as cleverly managed sabotage. That last incident of an aggressive servo was remarkable. I was the one who met Dick Smythe right after he was attacked, and the incident marked a new turn in the pattern — the servo acting while plugged into the power point though the power was not switched on.

'I gave old Dick a helping hand, then rushed to Archnov's flat to tell him about it. He was pretty well floored by the news, just didn't know what to make of it and looked very worried.'

Clemence stood in readiness to depart. 'I must be off to my cubby-hole of an office to write up the current health of our wonder society,' he said. Then, as if struck by an afterthought, he added: 'I enjoyed chatting with you. It was good to meet someone of my own generation. How about dropping into the social club this evening for a glass? I take it that, as an old guardsman, you don't object to a drink.'

'Never yet been known to refuse one,' said Hynes, grinning. 'What time?'

'Oh, let's say about quarter to eight. We can tell each other the usual tall tales about what we did in the war.'

'Fine. I'll be ready when you are.'

Clemence went on his way, leaving Hynes to finish his coffee. The detective liked Clemence, who had so much in common with himself. He was one with whom he could bond in the easy way of those with a shared experience of war.

He was plainly a valuable contact because he constantly checked the pulse of New Society with the skill of a professional. He watched the moods and nuances of the community. His knowledge of Archnov's background was highly interesting, and he would doubtless be useful in supplying data on remaining top academics in New Society.

Briefly, Hynes regretted having to keep up the deceit of being Edgar Herford, a writer researching a project. He would have preferred to be totally honest with Clemence about his real identity and his purpose in New Society; but he had agreed to act the part assigned to him in the procedure plotted by Sir Elkanah Artingstall, and could only adhere to it.

Leaving the restaurant, he walked through strengthening spring sunshine, heading for his apartment without knowing what he would do for the rest of the morning. He mused over Archnov's career as Clemence had relayed it from the professor's own account. Abruptly, he stopped and stood still, frowning, as if smitten by a particularly absorbing thought.

'Hmmm!' he muttered. Then he repeated a portion of Ted Clemence's utterance just before they parted: ' . . . *tall tales about what we did in the war.*' As if playing back a half-forgotten film in his brain, he tried to recall portions of briefings on the unfolding world war he had sat in on when seconded to the secret army nerve-centre in Baker Street.

After a short space, he tightened his mouth into a determined line, then resumed walking with a quickened pace.

Reaching his flat, he made at once for the telephone. Each flat was equipped with a phone and, inevitably, they were linked to Auntie. Hynes had never used his phone before and it was not fitted with a dial. A warm and gentle female voice asked for the number he required when he put the instrument to his ear. He naturally thought of the voice as that of Auntie, and wondered if she could listen in to his conversation. The voice was friendly and docile, and he wondered if this cunningly covered a secret brooding. Was the artificial brain on the hill plotting a new act of revolt?

He asked for the number of his London home. Miss Tilly Budd sounded surprised at hearing from him, and showed her usual concern for him mixed with the grave dignity which he believed cloaked the fact that she was half in love with him.

'Mr Hynes! What a surprise! Where are you, and are you safe and well? Not collecting broken bones and black eyes again, I hope.'

'I'm quite safe and well and comfortable in the Western Isles. Now listen, my good Miss Budd, I want you to do some research in our library. On the bottom set of shelves of modern books there's a brand new set of war histories. I want you to look up some items in one or two of them. So collect your shorthand notebook and take some notes. I'll give you a list of what I need to know. Call me at this number with the results of your research as soon as you finish it.'

He proceeded to dictate a long string of detailed questions, knowing that the faithful Miss Budd would be recording them in her impeccable shorthand and, with her pride in her almost clockwork competence, would supply him with every last detail he required.

After more than half an hour's wait, the phone rang. He snatched up a notebook and pen to record what his secretary had to tell him.

For ten minutes, he jotted down notes from the information she supplied. He queried three or four points and soon had a full set of answers to the questions he posed. As their conversation concluded, Miss Budd said, in her ever-dutiful style: 'I would never dare ask what you are doing so far away, Mr Hynes, but I sincerely hope you will not return in a smashed-up condition.'

'I shall not, Miss Budd,' he responded as he replaced the receiver. Then he read through the notes he had made, gave a grunt of satisfaction, and said aloud: 'But I think you have given me the ammunition to begin smashing up someone else pretty severely.'

And he tightened his mouth into an even more determined line.

7

Rogue Servos

The evening at the social club in the company of Ted Clemence proved pleasantly relaxing. A convivial crowd of men and women gathered there in a warm atmosphere hung with cigarette smoke and alive with bright chatter. Most of those present were on the sunny side of life, and there was a freshness of spirit in the air. Several of the young women showed that island life had not removed them from fashionable trends, and they made attractive pictures in dresses of the 'New Look' style now becoming all the rage in the wider world.

Anxieties about Auntie's recent haywire behaviour seemed to be on hold. Backing the chattering and the laughter, a juke-box played up-to-the-minute popular ditties: *Nature Boy*; *South America, Take It Away*; and *Peg o' My Heart*. In addition to the chance to sit back with a glass in his hand, Hynes made the acquaintance of a section of New Society's personnel through Clemence's introductions; and, in the flow of conversation, momentarily forgot some preoccupying considerations sparked off by the information newly supplied by Tilly Budd.

The evening fled quickly, and Hynes and Clemence left the club together to walk back to their apartments just as the first shades of night fell, with the air holding spring balminess as well as the ever-present invigorating saltiness of the sea. They strolled directly into an unexpected drama.

No other people were about as they passed some undeveloped land just beyond the club building. It was a wild tract of coarse grass bordering the paved footway and sweeping up to a hillock topped by some stunted shrubbery. With startling suddenness, there was a stirring on the crest of the hillock and, out of the shrubbery, like a jungle beast breaking cover, there emerged a servo.

It trundled down the sloping ground at an astonishing speed with its arms flailing, and it was followed by a second, and then a third. All came out of a gap in the shrubbery and moved with a remarkably sure stability over the rough surface of the grass. The two men stopped in their tracks and stood in momentary paralysis as they realised that the mechanical devices were coming straight for them.

Although they had no faces to signal their mood or intentions, the servos gave the impression of bearing a malignant animosity towards Hynes and Clemence; and before the two could take to their heels, the initial three speeding devices came off the slant of land and barged into them with whirling arms. Then three more came off the crest of the rise and followed the first trio at speed.

Clemence received a powerful blow to the head and was sent reeling, trying to keep his balance. A second servo charged in and joined the first in raining a series of blows on Clemence, while Hynes, in the midst of an attempt to reach his companion and fight the aggressive devices with his bare hands, was assailed by another pair of servos with swinging arms. Striking with a determination and an accuracy suggesting they were sentient creatures, they beat at Hynes until he was bent almost double, covering his head with his arms, trying to protect himself.

Clemence went down and rolled on the pavement. In this lower position, he was out of the reach of the flailing arms, but the two servos kept charging him with their wheeled bases, thumping into his ribs and legs.

Meanwhile, Hynes, breathless and bruised by the continual torrent of blows, had no idea how many servos were attacking him. It felt as if the whole world was suddenly full of savage and vengeful living entities. He almost buckled at the knees, but somehow managed to retain his balance as he tried to fight off the violent blows with bare fists: determined to keep the servos from bringing him down and giving him the same treatment Clemence was suffering. There was such precision and purpose about the attack that Hynes had the eerie feeling that the wholly mechanical and electronically-powered creations were acting as if they were living creatures gifted with powers of thought and reason.

He dropped under the raining blows to a near-squatting position, hoping to make a grab at the base of one of the servos, thinking that if he could pull the thing down and off the stability of its wheeled base it would be immobilised, resembling a beetle lying helplessly on its back with its legs twitching in the air.

Then, abruptly, the device drew back swiftly before his fingers could close on a reachable part of its structure. Its arms ceased flailing and fell immobile. It suddenly whirled around to change direction, then rolled off the paved way back to the stretch of grassland, and began trundling off in the direction from whence it came.

In the background, Clemence rolled over, seeming to ache in every part of it's body. Dimly, he realised that the servos had ceased their attack.

He held his head in his hands while he

tried to get his dizzy consciousness in order, and saw that the aggression had halted abruptly and all the servos were drawing away from the scene of the violent action. Hynes was still on his feet, staggering around, trying to regain his balance. Behind him, the robotic devices were retreating, progressing back up the slope of land in single file, moving quickly like a squad of soldiers in some military action.

Gasping heavily, feeling defeated and without the energy to pursue the servos — for whatever good that might do — he moved over to Ted Clemence, who was trying to rise to a standing position.

'Are you all right?' he called as he shambled towards his companion.

'I think so,' said Clemence shakily. 'Bruised and cut a bit here and there, but I reckon there's no harm done. What did you make of that performance?'

'Search me, but it was something entirely new,' responded Hynes, squinting at the top of the rise of land where the last of the servos was disappearing through the line of shrubbery. 'Those servos were not like the ones that attacked the Lindleys' baby, or the one that tackled Dick Smythe. Those were at least plugged into the power points of the houses — but this bunch were independent of any points or any cables, charging around in the open air instead of being confined indoors. Those servos have been doctored in some way. They've been turned from household devices into aggressive beasts.'

Clemence was bending, ruefully examining a tear in the leg of his trousers. 'Professor Archnov must be told about this,' he said. 'Maybe something like this has happened elsewhere. Possibly this was only one instance of several, and Auntie has launched the big revolt everyone has feared but shoved to the back of their minds.' He turned and saw that Hynes was trekking up the grassy bank on unsteady legs, following the path of the now-disappeared servos.

Hynes reached the straggle of shrubbery at the crest. It was close to full night now, and the moon appeared only sporadically from behind banked clouds now and again. From the rise, he could make out only a sweep of land beyond the hillock. There was no sign of the servos. In the uncertain light, he could discern a corner of a small white building poking out from the dark line of some trees. From what little he had learned of the geography of New Society, he recalled that there were small outstations of Auntie planted at various points. They were power stations essential to the smooth running of the electronic brain's multitudinous services. The disappeared servos could only have entered that building.

He narrowed his eyes, looked at the sweep of the land, and tried to gauge exactly where this point of the island was. So far as he could make out, the loch was a little way to the north with the airstrip close to it. Beyond the loch lay the unguarded end of the great fence that had intrigued him from his arrival on the island. At that point, only a cluster of high rocks stood between New Society, and the stony beach and open sea. He came down the land thoughtfully.

Clemence asked: 'See anything? Are those servos still anywhere about?'

'No, they've totally disappeared. The whole affair is a complete puzzle.' Hynes said nothing about seeing the outstation, or his suspicion that the servos had entered it.

'I keep wondering if Auntie has sprung any more of those tricks elsewhere,' murmured Clemence. 'I'd like to patch myself up after this little caper and fall into bed, but I think we should call on Archnov and put him in the picture. If Auntie really is off her rocker, there might have been outbreaks of trouble all over New Society. Archnov's flat is not too far from here.'

Hynes nodded agreement and the pair, feeling the effects of their punishing experience, walked off towards the professor's residence.

They reached the flat, located in another residential block, rang the doorbell and Archnov opened the door. He was stripped to the waist and holding a towel.

He looked surprised to find Hynes and

Clemence standing there, showing signs of their ill-usage by the servos. He greeted them with some attempt at his old heartiness. 'Didn't expect visitors at this time of night. Sorry to be in a state of undress. I had just stepped out of the bathroom when you rang.'

Frowning, he saw the cuts and abrasions on the faces of the two; then, as if he had thought of something important, he made a hasty, self-conscious movement, slinging the towel over his right shoulder so that it covered the upper part of his bare right arm. Hynes noted the deliberateness of the action and the quick, sly glance Archnov threw directly at him. In spite of the electric light flooding the room, the professor's face held a noticeable pallor, emphasising the peculiar birthmark in the centre of his forehead, and there was eloquence in that fleeting, furtive glance. It was querying whether Archnov had been caught out in the move with the towel. But the detective had already noticed, with a startled and chilling sense of near-horror, the set of tattooed letters and numbers on the arm which Archnov's speedy action had been meant to conceal. Though Hynes had glimpsed them momentarily, he knew only too well what they signified.

He strove to maintain an unruffled demeanour after seeing the characters inked into the professor's flesh, and his surprise seemed not to have registered with Archnov.

'Sorry to bother you at this hour, Professor,' said Hynes with a deadpan face. 'We've just had a strange experience. It looks as if Auntie's behaving oddly again. We were attacked by aggressive servos. They were running about in the open, quite detached from any power points. We wondered if you've had any word of anything else of the sort happening.'

Archnov stared with round eyes and an open mouth, his face clouded.

'Really? That's almost unbelievable news. No, I haven't heard of anything else of that kind — at least, not yet. You look as if you've had a pretty rough time of it. You chaps obviously had a fearful scragging. It's a frightfully disturbing development. It comes on the heels of rumours of people being scared of trusting their cars to Auntie for steering, and a general fear of servos. Do come in and tell me more.'

It was plain that, after being caught off-balance when his tattoo was briefly exposed, he had quickly recovered his character pose, and his schoolboy jargon was back on display.

Hynes and Clemence stepped into the professor's comfortable flat. 'Take a seat,' said Archnov. 'Excuse me. I must put a shirt on. And it might be a good idea to go over to Dr Willis at the dispensary afterwards and let him dress those cuts and bruises.' He strode for a bedroom door, keeping the towel clamped to his right shoulder with his left hand.

Minutes later, Hynes and Clemence were relating the tale of their waylaying and attack by the servos but Hynes now had reason to fully conceal what he had seen from the hillock after the fight. He said only that he had seen nothing of the servos since, and mentioned nothing of the outstation that served Auntie's control of New Society's daily life — nor of his half-belief that the rogue servos had

111

entered the building.

Archnov posed some probing questions. 'You were attacked near the stretch of open land near the social club, you say?'

'Yes, just off the pathway where there is a small hill with some bushes on its top,' Ted Clemence told him.

'I know the spot. And the business with the Lindleys' baby and the attack on Dick Smythe occurred indoors in the housing colony. Then there was the mishap with Lindley's car, which happened in the middle of the roadway at a point I know well.' The professor scratched his ear, ruminated for a moment, then added: 'I'm becoming interested in just where incidents of Auntie's malfunctions show up. Locations might indicate where in the big brain there are faults. Just as portions of the human brain are responsible for an individual's faculties and behaviour, portions of Auntie's brain govern bits of the map she controls. I must get my people to continue looking at Auntie in detail, but with more emphasis on the location aspect. This matter of servos charging

112

about in the open and attacking people is a frightfully bad development. Auntie's eccentricities are growing worse. We must stop them somehow, or all of New Society could collapse. I hear there are already rumbles of discontent in some quarters.'

Hynes noted the anxiety written on the professor's face. For the first time, he was not deflecting worries about Auntie's performance with thin platitudes, declaring that there was little to be concerned about and everything would turn out right. The detective also caught a couple of sidelong glances from Archnov as if he was dubious about knowledge Hynes might have absorbed during this visit to his apartment. In truth, Hynes had taken in one disconcerting fact but maintained his poker-faced demeanour, revealing nothing.

With Clemence, he prepared to leave and both assured Archnov that they would tend their abrasions and bruises themselves without bothering Dr Willis, the settlement's medical man.

They walked through the night towards their accommodation block, vigilantly aware that more aggressive servos might emerge out of the night but none appeared. They discussed the attack they had just endured and the disturbing new aspect of the servos' behaviour, the fact they ran loose in the open instead of being confined indoors and restrained by a cable plugged into a power supply.

Yet again, Hynes wished he could be open with Clemence and reveal his true identity and his assignment in New Society. He liked the tall, young ex-pilot and knew he could be a good ally in a tight corner.

And, even as he walked, he was contemplating a course of action that could land him in a tight corner.

8

Encounter by Night

Night enfolded New Society and all was silent when Hereward Hynes stealthily exited his flat. He took pains to close the door of his apartment soundlessly, not wishing to disturb Ted Clemence, sleeping next door. He walked quietly along the dimly lit corridor to the main door of the building and slipped out into the night.

Hynes had cleaned up his abrasions with dabs of iodine here and there. Like Clemence he had not received any substantial injury from the rough handling by the servos but he ached considerably. Such street lights as New Society had were subdued and the spring night was dark and slightly chilled by the wind from the sea.

The surroundings were without any sign of life and the windows of all the nearby domiciles were dark. Hynes, always conscious of the possibility of marauding servos, walked quickly, retracing the way to the spot where he and Clemence were attacked. He reached that point, feeling a more marked strength in the sea-wind through being so much closer to the unguarded end of the fenced-off settlement.

His mind was on the small building partially shielded by trees he had noted from the top of the rise and, knowing this was a locality where servo activity was thickest, he walked gingerly up the rise, trying to watch all sides at once. All remained peaceful as he reached the crest. Soldier-like, he lay on the grass to keep concealed and, as best he could, he surveyed the dark hollow lying beyond the hump of land.

The corner of the building was only just discernible in the midst of a shadowy mass of untamed grass, shrubbery and wind-stunted trees. Again, there was nothing in the way of human life or rogue servos to be seen. He rose and cautiously made his way down into the hollow, heading for the visible corner of the

116

building and reasoning that there must be a doorway on a side of the building which was out of view from the vantage point he had just vacated. A fugitive moon appeared very briefly, spread a moment of silver light then disappeared behind heavy clouds.

From his pocket he produced a small but powerful electric torch, a regular addition to the requirements he took when travelling on a mission. He used its beam to aid his progress over the thickly grown wild grass and tangles of vegetation under his feet. He reached the small building, went to one side and, sure enough, found a narrow doorway. Its wooden door was open and the torch showed him a stout branch, fallen from a tree, used as a wedge to keep it open.

He swept the ground around the doorway with the beam of the torch and saw that there was a pathway of flattened vegetation leading from the building towards the rising land. It was heavier than any traces that could have been caused by Hynes' own walk over the terrain so it was plainly the track of the several servos that had attacked Hynes and Clemence, earlier that night. There was eloquent evidence of human interference at this site where the door of the small service station was jammed open to ensure that the servos could leave the station then return into it.

Hynes entered the open door, swinging the torch beam around him. He found he was in a compact chamber, with one wall covered by complicated looking dials and cables. He jumped when the light showed him a set of servos, standing like a row of soldiers just in front of him. They seemed to be intimidating him though they were faceless. Then he realised they were totally immobile and showed no signs of leaping into belligerent life.

He pierced the darkness behind them with the torch beam and found there were more of them, all standing stock-still. It was as if the place was a storehouse of servos. He was without any knowledge of electronic engineering or of cybernetics, the relatively new discipline of mechanical brains, but he investigated the bank of assorted dials and cables with the light of the torch, finding nothing that suggested any of the servos were plugged into anything in this outcrop of Auntie's guiding intelligence.

Then, as the light beam swept down, it showed a slight glitter on the floor. It was caused by the shine on some recently created metal filings left by some work on a stout metal pipe running under the banked dials. Hynes bent for a closer look and saw that, just above the tell-tale filings, a new-looking addition had been attached to the pipe — a metal housing holding a form of lens, somewhat like the cats' eyes studding New Society's roadways. More evidence of outside intervention, thought Hynes. Someone had been into this isolated outstation and carried out work on its equipment which very likely had something to do with the aggressive servos setting out and attacking Hynes and Clemence. Then he saw a second pair of neatly drilled holes, side by side beside the addition to the pipe. Again, his torch revealed another pile of new-looking metal fragments on the floor under the holes, further evidence of recent drilling.

Hynes went outside again to re-examine

the immediate vicinity of the entrance in the faint hope that he might find some clue to the intruder. The ground proved barren. Just as he moved a few yards away from the little building he heard a growing rustling as if someone was tramping through the vegetation. He quickly switched off his torch and saw a moving erratic light in the midst of the trees. Someone was approaching using an electric torch to pick out a path through the overgrown terrain just as Hynes had. He hoped the approaching person had not seen his torch beam.

The newcomer's light was suddenly quenched. Abruptly, a dark bulk hurled itself out of the darkness, taking Hynes wholly by surprise. He had the fleeting impression of a man wearing a trilby hat barging into him and knocking him breathless. He tried to retaliate, smote the man forcefully on the cheek just under his left eye but, immediately, a fist thudded into his jaw and he went spinning backwards, hitting the ground to lie flat on his back, momentarily senseless.

He had a dim perception of his attacker

fleeing from the vicinity, crashing his way through the undergrowth and shrubbery, retreating in the direction he came. He got to his feet unsteadily and stumbled around, looking for his lost torch and eventually finding it. Fighting for his breath and, in a befuddled way, he made an attempt to pursue the attacker, tripped over some straggling growths and almost fell then realised that course of action was hopeless. His attacker had too good a start on him. Hynes thought ruefully that the man in the trilby must have spotted his torch beam before he switched it off, so was alerted to act.

His brain was swimming in bewilderment and he sat down on the ground, trying to clear his thoughts. Whatever the identity of the man in the trilby, Hynes knew he had landed a fairly heavy blow on his face and it would surely leave a trace. As his consciousness cleared, he thought of the direction from which the man had approached. He had definitely come from within New Society and not from the location now at Hynes' back where the gap in the fencing could allow an intrusion from the sea. Given the small population of New Society, it should not be difficult to identify him before evidence of the blow subsided.

Hynes picked himself up feeling shaken but not wholly defeated. At least, he knew there were plain signs of interference with the electrical installation, part of Auntie's lifeblood, in the small outstation. And the newish glitter of the deposit of metal turnings he saw on the floor indicated it had occurred fairly recently.

It looked as though there was at least one man within the New Society community who had some connection with the manipulation of Auntie and he was on his way to the outstation when frightened away by the unexpected encounter with Hynes. Could he be the unknown saboteur responsible for causing Auntie to swerve so dramatically off her carefully calibrated course?

He moved around the ground over which he and the unknown man had tussled, shining torchlight around thinking there was a slim chance that his assailant had left some form of clue. It proved fruitless but, swinging the beam in the direction of the door of the outstation, he noted intriguing flattened tracks in the rough grass. They were caused by the group of servos that had marched out of the building then returned to it after attacking Ted Clemence and himself. But there was also the suggestion of the passage of another set of wheels, lighter and probably indicating the course of a single servo. They veered away from the door of the station and led into the darkness to Hynes' right.

Hynes knew that the darkness cloaked the trees behind which lay the loch and, a little way beyond that, the open end of the settlement's fence. Where the fence ended, there was the guardian barrier of rocks and then the stony beach and the sea.

Though still groggy after the struggle with the unknown man, he was curious about this newly discovered track which spoke plainly of a single servo having very recently made its way out of the small building and proceeded over the tangled ground, beating down the grass with its weight. Bending, he followed the track with torchlight. It went towards the trees then into a small clearing where there was soft, sandy ground. Here, the passage of something equipped with four wheels was marked distinctly in the sand.

Hynes remembered how the wheels on the servos he and Clemence fought were positioned and the tracks confirmed that this was definitely the trail of a single servo. It led him over sandy ground where it became indistinct now and again but was soon visible again and when Hynes flashed the torch on the terrain ahead, he caught sight of dark water and realised he was almost alongside the large pond which was locally referred to as a 'loch'. The tracks skirted the loch and were lost for a yard or so in rough grass but Hynes picked them up again on the dry and dusty surface of a dirt path, Probing the darkness ahead with the torch beam, he realised there was a humped structure only a short distance away, the kind of building familiar to all who had experience in the armed services — a Nissen hut.

He remembered how he spotted such a hut when he flew in with Alec McLeith and recalled that it was not far from the landing strip and close to where the island tailed off into the Atlantic. Indeed, he was aware of the salt-spiced breeze coming off the sea which drove off some of the weariness following his run-in with the man in the dark. The electric torch showed that the hut had a decrepit appearance and was without a door. The tracks of the servo plainly followed the path up to it.

Determinedly, he walked up to the hut and entered. Its gloomy inner cavern held a heavy smell of disuse and decay and his torch revealed it to be largely empty apart from some broken wooden boxes heaped in a corner; a rusted central stove, traditional in Nissens. It was bereft of its tubular metal chimney. There was some tattered matting on the floor and his torch beam lit up the woebegone smile of a forgotten blonde pin-up girl on one curved metal wall. Swinging the beam further, he found a larger wooden box. In front of it stood an old wooden chair of the 'general service' pattern supplied in barracks. It looked as if the box had been used as a desk. On top of it, Hynes found some tools: a file, several screwdrivers of varying sizes, some lengths of wiring, what appeared to be small electrical valves and some scattered oddments of devices apparently to do with electrical work although Hynes had no grasp of their purpose.

All these discoveries were untouched by age. Like the evidence of tampering with equipment in the outstation, they spoke of recent activity in this lonely, obscure portion of the map of Benarbor. Someone had used the large box as a workbench as he doubtless plotted ways of disrupting the workings of Auntie and throwing a figurative spanner into the works of New Society. He had worked to create additions to the power installations in the outstation and these, surely, affected the behaviour of the servos.

Hereward Hynes' investigative spirits were recharged as he recalled how he spotted from the air the weakness in New Society's tight security which could allow access to the university colony by means of the unfenced area close to the shore.

He knew he was close to that location

now and, spurred by curiosity, he made his way through wild shrubs and tangles of grass to where his torch showed him the fence ended and only large but not impassable rocks guarded the way to the sea. With torchlight illuminating his path, he picked his way through the rocks and set foot on the stony beach. The wind was stronger now and, without any great hope of finding anything, he splashed his torchlight around the pebbles of the narrow shoreline. It seemed a hopeless exercise but he was in search of some indication of a boat having landed at this point. He shrugged in disappointment then suddenly caught sight of a dark splotch contrasting with the white pebbles just above where the tide lapped the stony shore. It had dried but it certainly had the look of petrol.

Hynes rubbed his chin, thinking that a light boat with a slightly leaking outboard motor at her stern might have been hauled ashore here to keep it clear of the tide. The shelving nature of the shoreline meant there was no means of mooring it and, if left floating just offshore, it could drift out to sea. Was the person who came in from the sea the one who sabotaged Auntie, working in both the hut and the outstation? Or did several people come in from the sea and were involved in possible sabotage? However many were involved, their activities suggested they had a high degree of electronic skill.

And who was the man he fought near the outstation and where did he fit into Hynes' conjectured pattern of events? All he could be sure of was that he came out of New Society and retreated back into it — and he might be identified by a face bruised in the fight — so long as the mark remained visible.

With these questions on his mind, he left the shoreline and negotiated the line of rocks again. He made his way from this isolated and overgrown region of the island, down to the paved paths of New Society, again keeping an eye open for rampaging servos and the man he fought but seeing neither. With some alarm, he noticed the first silver of a new dawn streaking the wide sweep of sky and realised that an eventful night was almost over.

He did not see anyone as he walked through the housing section. He let himself into his flat noiselessly, tumbled into bed as the dawn widened. Feeling the effects of the two bouts of physical combat he had endured that night, he caught a few hours of turbulent sleep.

9

The Ragged Men

The boatyard stood on a spit of land a little way south of the town of Fort Calaige. It was in an isolated spot and there was an assortment of small boats anchored along its landing stage and several vessels were beached around a couple of tin-roofed sheds, one considerably larger than the other. It was in a picturesque location, backed by a wide sweep of Atlantic sky, with wheeling, screeching gulls to the seaward. To the landward side, there was a distant rise of purple hills. The yard had clearly seen better days and the indications were that not a great deal of business was done there.

In the larger of the sheds, a tall and lean man with a face that betrayed a history of hardship stood at a scarred old oaken table littered with tools and oddments of wood and metal. He was working on some objects with wires attached, suggesting they had to do with electricity.

His clothing was shabby and he might have been a labourer whose circumstances were modest. At the opposite side of the table stood three men, similar in type and costume to the lean man.

The door opened and another man who, in appearance, had much in common with the others, entered and walked towards the lean man. He fumbled in a pocket and produced a Scottish pound note and half a dozen coins and laid them on the table top.

'Here, Herr Doktor. Just a little to help out,' he said.

Acknowledging the gesture with a nod, the lean man said: 'Don't call me Herr Doktor. Those days are over, Stovic.'

'Maybe they are, but you are still worthy of your title. You're one of the most brilliant scientists ever to come out of the University of Vienna. Long ago, your nation feted you, August Richter. Nowhere was there greater regard for academic attainment than in pre-war Austria.'

The lean man made a sour face. 'That was before the nation disgraced itself and was carried away in an orgy of raised-arm salutes and swastika flags. Now I'm reduced to mere tinkering with what miserable equipment I can scrape together. Like Austria, I'm struggling.'

'Austria will recover. I'm confident of it. It's in a happier state than my poor country, Richter,' said the other gloomily.

'I sympathise with you, Stovic,' said Richter. 'But perhaps all will be put right in the Ukraine when the nations find proper stability after all the upheaval.'

The door swung open to let in a scrawny, shambling man who butted into the conversation at once.

'Proper stability will come when all greedy ambition is thwarted,' he intoned in a reedy, quivering tone. 'Greed for power; greed for land; greed for the gold in the treasuries of nations and all the greedy talk of building new philosophies of life and creating wonderfully attractive futures needs crushing. It's all folly. All is destined to end in dust and rubble as the Nazi dream ended and as the Soviet dream will end. Mark my words: the monstrous notion of a new Utopian technological society being worked out on the island yonder will cave in. And the misguided wealthy ones who finance such downright evil ideas might be brought to their senses . . . '

Richter cut him off in mid-flow. 'Damn you, Palachenko, when are you going to stop preaching like a zealot and do your bit by coughing up a few shillings to help out now and again?' he growled. 'Everyone else tries to put something into the pot but you're always pleading poverty. How do you think I can buy bits of equipment and petrol for the boat with my pockets nearly empty?'

'Well, labouring in a brick works doesn't make me rich,' whined Palachenko.

'The wages are not that small. And other people are in menial work but manage to contribute to our cause,' Richter snorted. 'You're not starving and I notice you don't go short of drink. The Scottish people don't know what vodka is but gin is a pretty good substitute and I know you get plenty of that, costly though it is. It strikes me you were imbibing before you found your way over here.'

'A man must have some recreation. After what we put up with, year in and year out who is to blame any of us if we have a drink or two now and again?' countered Palachenko. 'It's easy enough for you. You have your experimenting to keep you happy and you've fallen on your feet, landing a job looking after a boatyard whose boss is away for months at a time. All on the strength of working on boats with your grandfather on an almost unknown Austrian river when you were a kid. What was the term the soldiers in the ordnance depot used? A cushy number? Yes, you got a cushy number when they let us loose from the months of hauling and lifting army supplies. Sometimes it was nearly as bad as being back in a Nazi forced labour camp.'

'Nonsense. The obligatory term of labouring for the army gave us a chance to be free civilians again,' said Richter. 'You should be grateful you were liberated by the British and not the Russians, which would hardly be liberation at all and you know it.'

Another newcomer slipped in through the door, a man in nondescript clothing, and, like the others, bony and worn by ill-use. He had the stolid face of a middle-European farmer but something about him suggested a man familiar with books. He dropped a few banknotes on the table.

'Just a little to help with whatever is needed most, Richter,' he said.

'Thank you, Grosz,' said the man at the table, working with a small screwdriver on an electrical fitting in his hand. In the next few minutes another four men entered and each dropped some money on the table in front of Richter as if contributing to a charity.

'And what is the latest move?' Grosz inquired. 'Did you improve the performance of the remote control?'

'Yes, at least to a degree. It's impossible to be sure how plans work out when you can't observe results at first hand. Much of it is hit and miss but I know the car on the road responded and the initial household servos I tried out worked according to plan. Last night I set several servos loose on New Society. They were specially adapted to my latest standard and pretty aggressive. Returning signals suggested they romped around and possibly scared some people who were at large. However, making cars and servos misbehave might scare some people over there into deserting the project but it is merely inflicting pinpricks. Maybe it will undermine faith in the brain and the professor's reputation, too. But I have plans to do that for good and all.'

Grosz stroked his chin thoughtfully. 'I confess to having a bad conscience about sending cars off course. If it causes some undeserving person to be injured or even killed, the justice of our actions would be diminished in the eyes of the public. From what you say, this interference with serving robots has results that are not very precise.'

'That's so and I'm not too happy about it,' responded Richter, 'but my crude remote service device tells me my intervention is causing servos to go into the attack even if I do not know whom they are attacking. Anyway, the whole business is bound to make a mess of the total brain project. As you know, I've made numerous trips over to the island and worked there out of the way of the main centre of activity. Having perfected my methods of tapping into the brain, I can now activate them by remote control to create maximum disruption but I need to be on the island with my equipment to do it.'

Grosz scratched his head. 'I suppose, being just a simple and peaceable professor of philosophy, I'll never understand how you achieve this remote control business — how you tap into the electronic brain and make it do what it is not programmed to do.'

'I'm not sure I know myself,' Richter said. 'I have to delve into memories of work I did when young and dredge up recollections of theories and experiments I've all but forgotten or which were almost driven out of me by the wretched treatment we all endured these last few years.' He paused, lifted his head to glower at the shed's small window, beyond which there was a dim line of land, lying across a stretch of sea — the coastline of the isle of Benarbor upon which Richter bestowed a frowning, malevolent glare.

'I suppose,' resumed Richter, 'I kept my hopes alive during captivity by trying to mentally rewrite the contents of the report on my most advanced approaches in cybernetics. It was stolen from me by a cocky young student.

'That was during a strange time when we in Austria entertained students from Kiev University and the thief is at this moment not a million miles from Benarbor. Anyway, probing into the big brain and throwing it off course is done by employing a technique something like a sonar device that searches a deep ocean for sounds and eventually hits on the presence of a submarine. Only it's not the throbbing human life of deep-sea sailors one encounters but the throbbing of electrically induced thoughts coursing around the innards of a man-made creation.'

'An unnatural abomination, flying in

the face of nature — that's what that wretched creation on yonder island is!' spluttered Palachenko who had been brooding in the background. 'It will never improve the world. It crouches there, ticking over, simply awaiting the day it will bring destruction down on those who devised it. Because that is exactly what will happen if humanity puts its trust in some device that regulates life like clockwork. Pretty soon, man himself will behave like clockwork. Haven't we seen enough of clockwork men with blank faces, goose stepping like clockwork, flinging up their arms in salutes like clockwork and chanting the praises of their Fuhrer like clockwork?'

'Be quiet, Palachenko,' said Richter sharply. 'You preach too much and, in any case, that day of reckoning you're always foretelling will occur very soon.'

The dialogue employed by these men was in keeping with their almost vaga-bond appearance. It was a sometimes stumbling amalgam of a commonly shared German with oddments of Rus-sian, Serbo-Croat and Polish with a

modicum of French, a language understood over a wide area of Europe. It was
the polyglot argot of the hordes of men of
many nationalities who were forced to live
crowded together for years as enslaved
labourers of both the Nazis and the
Russians. War's end made them into DPs
— Displaced Persons who could not
return to their own countries where the
vagaries of war had installed governments
violently opposed to the ideals of this vast
tide of human flotsam.

Post-war, whether liberated by Allied
forces or having escaped from captivity,
they were collected in camps in Germany
and their physical health and political
affiliations were probed. If the British
rules of DP clearance were met, certain
groups were permitted to enter the UK,
live in camps attached to units of the
armed forces and after a year or so of
labouring with either the army or air
force, could remain in the country and
become part of the civilian population.
Ideally, it was hoped this influx of willing
labour would help rebuild a country
battered and weakened by the war.

The handful of men clustering around Richter came out of that human tide. From the German holding camp, they were deployed to an army ordnance base in north-west Scotland and had only recently concluded their obligatory labour contracts. Entering into civilian life, they found the region had little industry offering a chance of employment save the brick works. Though others drifted to the more heavily industrialised region of Glasgow, there was a group surrounding ex-Professor August Richter who chose the brick works for a particular reason. They sought vengeance for the brutal destruction of their pre-war lives and careers and the years of unrelenting labour for totalitarian regimes.

While working with the army, this group were alerted to what they considered a duty by the discovery of a long article in a popular magazine. It described a novel experiment taking shape on the island of Benarbor. It was to be a new approach to social planning, foreshadowing the future; a social entity guided by a huge electronic brain. There were photographs of building in progress, of the wealthy industrialist who poured funding into the scheme and of the leader of the project, a Professor Feodor Archnov. A character profile, accompanied by a photograph, described Archnov as a brilliant refugee, lucky enough to escape and spend the war years in Britain on hush-hush work for the government.

This description and portrait created dark anger and a thirst for retribution among the DP labourers. For they knew this man under another name and were well aware of the work he was truly engaged in during the war. They knew, too, they did not mistake his identity. The square birth mark in the middle of his forehead distinguished him completely.

Piankowski, a Pole, spoke up. 'What do you mean, Richter, when you say a day of reckoning will occur soon?'

Richter jerked his head towards the dim line of Benarbor beyond the window pane. 'A day of decisive reckoning for the learned professor yonder,' he said. He reached into his jacket pocket and produced a black Luger pistol which he held up in front of the company.

'You all know what this is,' he stated

grimly. 'I propose some real action. Don't ask me how I acquired this little toy but a fact of life in the British Isles today is the flourishing black market. Even here in remote Scotland you'll find the gentlemen called 'spivs' who can supply anything for a price. I'm contemplating a decisive move two days from now. The day will be the fifth anniversary of the shootings at Trolinka — don't you remember that spring day in 1943?'

There were scowls and angry rumblings among the gathered men.

'Remember it? How can we ever forget it?' said Stovic, the Ukrainian.

'Never!' declared Piankowski, the Pole, forcefully. 'A dozen men cut down by machine gun fire — some mere peasants and others intellectuals of brilliant promise but all good men.'

'And who manned his machine gun with more bloody minded enthusiasm than any other guard?' asked Richter in a low, brooding voice.

'We know who,' said another of the group. 'We know only too well.'

'I propose to mark that anniversary by

taking a couple of men over to the island — the boat cannot hold too many — and I'll set off confusion by putting the brain into a state of frantic misbehaviour. That will give us cover for our business with the professor. Stovic and Piankowski, I select you two if you're willing. You were both soldiers and you have guts and I'm not suggesting that any of the rest of you lack guts.'

'I'm willing,' said both Stovic and Piankowski in eager unison.

'Good, then I'll brief you later,' said Richter, returning the Luger to his pocket.

There were disappointed mutterings from others in the group. All these representatives of a large category of ill-used victims of war, now being rapidly forgotten as peacetime found its pace, had bitter resentment in their hearts. A role in the action on the island planned by Richter would assuage some of that bitterness. But Richter was their accepted leader and all were willing to bide by his decisions.

10

Discontent

Hynes, still feeling battered after the previous night's tussles with the warlike servos and the aggressive stranger near the outstation, was up early and breakfasted while there were yet few people in the restaurant.

He saw nothing of his close neighbour Ted Clemence since rising and, as he sat alone at a table, he could hear the conversation of a group of men at the next table. He recognised them as workers in the, to him, mysterious field of electronics, whose business was keeping Auntie running smoothly every day. There was subdued anger in the tone of their conversation and one, a man with a dark, scowling face, seemed to be particularly bitter.

'It looks as if Archnov is panicking. He might well call his meeting this morning but if he suggests these problems with

Auntie are due to negligence by the likes of us, I'll give him a piece of my mind,' he said. 'We've always done our jobs properly and we're as baffled as he is. If Auntie really is failing completely, I'm damned if I'll take any blame.'

'Quite right, Sid,' declared the man next to him. 'If anyone's to blame, I reckon it's the bunch of boffins in charge of this whole show. It strikes me they're living in fairly cushy style while all those wonderful promises of a slick new lifestyle are proving pretty thin. You wouldn't get me trusting a car linked to Auntie's cat's eye steering system after that dangerous business with young Lindley's car.'

'And there's no faith in the servos any more since Lindley's baby was attacked,' put in a third man. 'I suppose you've heard the whisper that a couple of blokes were attacked by servos last night? The whole project is falling to bits. I'm thinking of finding a safe job on the mainland.'

Hynes rose and approached the next table with an expression of bland innocence.

'Excuse me, gentlemen, did I hear

mention of a meeting this morning?' he asked.

The dark, scowling man looked up. 'Ah, Mr Herford, it looks as if something meaty for your book is developing. Haven't you heard? Professor Archnov has called a meeting in the recreation hall at ten this morning. The people at the top are alarmed by Auntie's failures and many of us lesser beings are becoming fed up with the way New Society is turning out. The notion that Auntie is somehow being sabotaged is floating around and we're all damned sure none of the workforce is to blame.'

'Sounds as though there's a little unease in the air,' said Hynes.

'Unease?' muttered the man named Sid. 'It'll be outright revolution if things don't change for the better.'

'Ten o'clock in the recreation hall. I'll be there,' said Hynes.

He returned to his table, finished his breakfast and was on his way out of the restaurant when he met Ted Clemence coming in.

'I overslept a bit. I suppose last night's

antics are to blame,' said Clemence.

'How do you feel?' asked Hynes.

'A bit stiff, otherwise all right — but I wouldn't want last night's trouble all over again.'

Hynes jerked his head to indicate the men at the table behind him.

'Speaking of trouble, there are some rumblings from the fellows at that table. There's some disillusion due to Auntie's behaviour and even talk of quitting for a job on the mainland.'

'I've been expecting it,' said the sociologist. 'The indications have been in the wind for some time. For a start, the novelty of a cybernetic controlled society was bound to fade after a while and there is no doubt that Auntie's performance is being interfered with to make things worse. Then there is the natural stifling effect of being more or less imprisoned behind a fence on a remote island. As a model for a harmonious social entity, I'm afraid New Society has some failings. Let's hope there are no hothead agitators in the ranks ready to spring into action.'

Hynes had resolved to keep quiet about

148

his discoveries in the outstation and the Nissen hut as well as the mystery of the man with whom he fought and his discovery of signs of a boat recently visiting the island. He said simply: 'If you haven't heard, Archnov has called a meeting for ten this morning in the recreation hall. I'll see you there.'

The recreation hall was a structure offering relaxation to the dwellers in New Society. Inside, there was a large space with tables for billiards and snooker at one end and ample room for indoor tennis, badminton, other sports as well as dancing. Meetings of various kinds were also held there and at ten that morning, it was almost totally full of New Society folk, all seated on chairs that had been set out by the hall's maintenance staff.

A long table had been set up at one end of the hall and behind it sat Professor Archnov, flanked by the top boffins of the experimental society.

Hereward Hynes arrived just before the hour and spotted Ted Clemence in a seat close to the front rank with a vacant chair beside him which Hynes quickly occupied.

149

He determined that, even with Clemence, whom he trusted, he would keep silent about what occurred during his return to the vicinity of the outstation the previous evening.

'Archnov looks rattled,' whispered Clemence. 'The troubles with Auntie seem to be becoming a burden.'

Hynes nodded and ran his eye along the line of assembled top academics. With Archnov were Thorne, the prissy Estcourt, the mostly silent Jones and straggly moustached Glassman. *Glassman!*

Hynes took another look at Glassman. There was something unusual about him. He kept his head turned to one side as if determined to keep the left side of his face out of view. He could not keep his face permanently turned from the audience, however, and had eventually to face the front of the hall. As he did so, he hastily held his hand up to his left cheek and kept it there. But, for a moment, he revealed the darkly discoloured weal under his eye.

Hynes reacted with surprise. Unless, by coincidence, he had received the bruise by some other means, it was the usually detached and scholarly-looking Glassman with whom he had struggled near the outstation the night before and who proved so powerful an adversary!

Hynes kept Glassman in view as Archnov stood to open the meeting. Obviously conscious that the bruise on his face was very noticeable, he tried to keep it concealed as much as possible. Doubtless, Glassman realised that the man who smote him could well be somewhere in the New Society community and could attest to his presence in the neglected and wildly overgrown region of the settlement.

Archnov was speaking in a voice that now and again quivered with edgy emotion.

'I've been hearing of people becoming disillusioned with New Society because of recent difficulties,' he said. 'Admittedly, it is proving difficult to pin down what is wrong but our team of special experts is working hard to detect and overcome the . . . '

'And getting nowhere, Professor — getting exactly nowhere!' hooted an interrupting

151

voice. Hynes saw that the dark, disgruntled man from the restaurant was on his feet. 'You've been promising progress for days. I'm one of the team trying to pinpoint the trouble and I know we're totally baffled.'

'That's right!' called another voice. 'More than one of us is ready to quit New Society. We're scared to trust our cars to Auntie's steering and she's even involved in the telephone system. How do we know she's not listening in — spying on us?'

There was an aggressive grumbling within the hall. The militant mood was clearly taking hold. Then the voice of a woman was heard, furthering the discontent: 'He's right! My husband and I feel the same way. After what happened to the Lindleys' baby, how can we be sure it's safe to bring up children here? I suppose you know that people are scared of their servos starting up of their own accord and are now unplugging them and laying them on their sides, off their wheels, so they can't rush around causing damage.'

'We were told this project was a pioneering effort we'd all be proud to be associated with but the whole show is blowing back on itself,' shouted another man. 'Whether the problems with Auntie started within herself or whether they were introduced by some kind of outside interference, I'm sick of the tension and uncertainty. I'm pretty close to giving up. Are you fellows really putting in the effort to clear up the problems? Maybe you boffins are just putting on a show and sitting back, living the high life at the expense of the University of Central UK?'

Archnov flushed almost purple and lost his temper. 'That's a grossly insulting statement!' he roared. 'We're all working conscientiously in the best interests of New Society!'

Ted Clemence leaned to one side to address Hynes in a low voice. 'That caught him on the raw. This could easily turn into a free fight. We're witnessing a crisis point in the short history of our brand new futuristic society.'

Hynes nodded. He still watched Glassman who, like his fellow boffins, was glowering ahead with an indignant expression. He had ceased to guard his bruised cheek and the vivid mark was plain to be seen. Hynes' thoughts returned to the incident of the previous night. He wondered about Glassman's purpose in being in the vicinity of the outstation. Did he know about the evidence there of someone drilling into the connection to Auntie, presumably to affect the brain's performance and the behaviour of the servos? With his technical education, he would doubtless fully understand its meaning.

Was he responsible for the drilling and therefore the elusive unknown saboteur whom some believed to be active in New Society? He certainly had not been inside the little building before Hynes investigated its interior, and Hynes was fairly certain that he had newly arrived on the scene when he so suddenly launched his attack; but had he been into the outstation at an earlier date, and was he in any way associated with whoever had visited the island by boat?

With one eye on Glassman, Hynes followed Archnov's speech and noted his demeanour. He was obviously shaken by the disturbed mood in New Society that

154

was manifestly spreading. His temper was becoming ragged now that some in the audience were voicing angry opposition.

'You really must be reasonable and give us some time to come to grips with our difficulties,' he pleaded. 'We're in the middle of a totally new experiment, one that's perhaps the only venture of its kind in the world. There are bound to be some growing pains. It's just a matter of having some patience.'

'Patience be damned!' yelled the disgruntled man from the restaurant. 'You and your brainy chums are taking long enough to cure things!'

He met a threatening, almost murderous glare from Archnov who looked for a moment as if he was going to lurch forward and attack the heckler.

'The professor really is losing his anchorage,' whispered Hynes to Clemence. 'He's losing his old school tie persona, too. Where's the jargon of the Lower Fourth at Greyfriars now?'

Privately, he thought the venomous glare he had just witnessed on Archnov's face was a graphic underlining of a truth about the professor he already possessed; but it was, for the moment, a truth he kept to himself.

After some further exchanges in which the growing antagonism of New Society's populace drove the boffins into a figurative corner, the meeting broke up with the boffins promising yet again to redouble their efforts to put New Society back on a smoothly running basis. Most of the participants, plainly unimpressed, left the hall with obvious simmering resentment.

Archnov and his companions looked as if they wished to beat a retreat to some bolthole as they tried to hasten through the departing crowd but Hynes managed to step into Dr Glassman's path as he made for the door.

'Sorry to see you've been given quite a thump in the face, Dr Glassman,' he commented. 'Have you been sparring with Bruce Woodcock in readiness for his next title fight?'

Glassman looked startled and gave Hynes a guilty look. For a moment he seemed lost for words then found his voice. 'No. I — er — I stumbled and bumped into the edge of a door,' he said. The quality of his fleeting expression of guilt confirmed for Hynes that Glassman knew whom he fought and who hit him in the darkness of the previous night.

They parted, each with a knowing glance at the other, a pair figuratively fencing with each other over a shared secret of which neither would speak. Hynes' mind once again returned to the puzzle surrounding Glassman and all the implications of his presence near the isolated outstation the previous night.

For Hynes the rest of the day was spent in spreading the notion that he was a literary man gathering material for a book. At different locations he spoke to individuals involved in various aspects of running New Society, from some of the technical experts to those in lesser but vital roles. He knew that Sir Elkanah Artingstall and the very top echelons of the University of Central UK would be delighted if he genuinely produced a book picturing New Society as an almost clinically clean, smoothly running social entity. It might be a captivating sales brochure for both New Society and Auntie who held it in her all powerful and benevolent care and was nanny and patron saint of a bright revolution in human relationships.

But his findings showed how far short of the ideal New Society had fallen. That morning's meeting showed in high relief the discontent that had been slowly growing in the island settlement. Auntie had lost her charms, was not trusted and even feared. There were those who had developed a nostalgic perspective and told Hynes that though they were enticed by life with Auntie at the start, the old-fashioned way of doing everything was preferable to the new-fangled New Society pattern of life.

'I can't understand why I fell for it all in the first place,' grumbled one man he interviewed. 'I suppose I wanted something new after being in the war. Now, I feel that what was good enough for my father would be good enough for me. I should never have given up my job in a Birmingham engineering shop.'

Such human feelings played a large

part in the discontent and there was another human dimension in the animosity which had surfaced against Archnov and his coterie of learned technical specialists. It was of the order of grumbling criticism which in other social contexts might be levelled at the boss or officer class. It had been well aired at the morning's meeting.

In the evening, Hynes met Ted Clemence in the social club for a drink and he mentioned to the sociologist the trend taken by the results of his questioning several New Society folk.

'Not one was fully satisfied,' he said. 'And there were several who told me they would leave the whole project and the island fairly soon.'

Clemence smiled. 'I know. I've watched the discontent grow for some time. Whether they came from Hampstead or the East End, Newcastle or Glasgow or sleepy Devon, many folk far prefer the old life they knew. You saw what the mood was at today's meeting. My next regular report will not make happy reading for the university bigwigs.'

Hynes sipped his beer. 'Yes,' he said thoughtfully. 'The meeting emphasised what you told me earlier, that you could see squalls developing.'

'And then some,' Clemence answered. 'Into the bargain, I have a very uneasy notion they'll arrive on our doorstep fairly soon.'

11

Invasion

It was early in the morning of the day when Dr August Ritcher planned his expedition to Benarbor, the anniversary of the day of the brutal action at Trolinka Camp in 1943, so distant in time and geography but vivid and fresh in the minds of the men gathering in the shed at the boatyard.

They were roughly clad and some wore elements of British army or RAF uniforms, donated by the forces for which they had laboured under contract. All were still finding their way in a new environment with a new freedom. Their faces were lean, bony and all were visible records of the harsh indignities they had suffered as the victims of war. Yet all had a dignity and a defiant determination that had never been crushed in their years of ill-treatment. These were DPs — Displaced Persons, a category of humanity wholly created by the savagery of the Second World War. They were proud of their stolid resilience and they wore the title of 'DP' as though it was the emblem of a gallant crack regiment.

As usual, Richter was standing at the table littered with technical equipment and the men gathered around him. There was an atmosphere of urgency among them.

'Are you determined to take only Piankowski and Stovic?' asked one of the men.

'I have no choice,' Richter said. 'I know you all want to get in on the action. You all contributed to plotting it and you deserve to go, but the boat is small. If it's overloaded, everything will end in disaster before we even reach the island.'

Palachenko pushed his way from the back of the group and walked unsteadily toward Richter. 'Disaster! That's the very thing I want to see. I want to be there when disaster engulfs the goings-on over on the island,' he declared thickly. 'Why can't I go with you? I was as good a soldier as any of you.'

'I don't deny that,' said Richter sharply, 'but, as I've just explained, the boat can't carry too many. Come to think of it, you were not at our last meeting when everything was settled. I suppose you were drinking somewhere. Anyway, we need clear and cool thinking and, frankly you, Palachenko, are a hothead. I believe you've been imbibing yet again, even this early in the day — and you're drunk!'

Palachenko stepped closer to Richter and glared at him. He teetered on his heels, recovered his balance and hooted: 'Not too drunk to be of any use. I wanted to be on hand to see the whole wretched society they've built on the island tumble down in ruins, as I warned their provider of money, old Artingstall, it would. I told him he was financing something that was at its heart opposed to the human spirit. A society based on a thinking machine can produce only unproductive idleness and minds ready to capitulate to any dangerous philosophy, no matter how fatuous. Haven't we seen enough of that sort of thing, Dr Richter

— human spirits capable of better things, brainwashed into hating and persecuting their fellow creatures?'

August Richter faced Palachenko with his lean face dark as a thundery sky and his hands balled into fists. He appeared ready to strike the loquacious Palachenko.

'You did *what*?' he spluttered. 'You talked to someone about what we are doing here? You don't mean you told someone about our secret plans?'

The eyes of all the company were on Palachenko and Richter's incredulity was mirrored on every face.

'I never divulged any secret plans,' stated Palachenko defiantly. 'I wrote to the old man, Artingstall, who put up the money for the project on Benarbor — sent two letters in fact, warning him that what he was backing was a dangerous scheme, bound to come to a bad end. And I don't regret it.'

'But why?' demanded Richter, now blank-faced with incomprehension.

'Yes, *why*?' called Udriakis, a pugnacious and short-tempered little Latvian.

Palachenko faced his fellows defiantly.

'I was determined to point out the error of his ways to him,' he told them in an unwavering voice though he wobbled on his feet drunkenly. 'The article that alerted us to the project on Benarbor included a detailed pen portrait of him. It said he worked his way up from poverty to become a major industrialist and he was always a humane and exemplary employer who cared about his workers. I was a poor boy myself once and I felt some sympathy for him. He is an old man and a good one. I felt he was donating his funds to a dubious cause and might be persuaded to think again. I sought out his home address and wrote to him. I did nothing to hinder the plans we make here.

'Aren't we living proof of the wickedness of twisted so-called sciences, leading to human beings being persecuted, enslaved and even herded into gas chambers because their philosophies, religions or ethnicity do not suit an evil dogma while so many of their fellow men marched blindly along, hypnotised as some dictator does their thinking for them — can't you see that a mechanical brain can become a kind of dictator if people become enslaved by it?'

The anger faded from Richter's face. He relaxed his bunched fists. He looked at Palachenko and recollected what he knew of him.

He was a Ukrainian. Like many among the tide of displaced persons, he had an intellectual bent and started out from poor peasant origins in the days of Soviet domination of the farmers. He worked to become a teacher, was fluent in several languages and had written some books and pamphlets which had antagonised the authorities. He was always a humanitarian. The brutal circumstances of his usage by those who enslaved him might have slightly unhinged him, made him eccentric and given him a fondness for the bottle but his tattered dignity was still intact, he was known to have the courage to challenge Soviet power by his writings and his instincts were honest and humane.

August Richter addressed the assembly in a voice now sympathetic to Palachenko. 'Forget any anger towards Mr Palachenko.

He acted unpredictably as usual, but what he did was not harmful to our plans. I believe every man here can understand his good intentions.'

There was a general murmur of agreement among the men and Richter told Palachenko with a suggestion of humour in his tone: 'Hard though it may be, you'll just have to accept that you're not sailing to the island — and you're still drunk!'

Ten minutes later, the whole company gathered on the landing stage of the boatyard and watched Richter, Stovic and Piankowski settle themselves into the small boat. The morning was fine, the sea was as calm as a millpond and the wind force was mild. The outboard motor was started and Richter steered the craft out into open water, leaving a curving wake behind it.

'There goes a landing party of three men with only one Luger pistol between them,' commented Udriakis. 'It's an unlikely invasion force. I only hope they know what they are doing.'

'I think they do,' said Grosz. 'I trust

Richter's intelligence and he briefed his two men very thoroughly yesterday. Even so, everything depends on his plans working out without any snags.'

The men on the landing stage watched the boat dwindle against the panoramic vista of the sea where the isle of Benarbor was a distant smudge on the far horizon; then they dispersed.

In the boat, Richter called over the *chug-chug* of the motor: 'When we land, stick together and follow me. We'll be in a very isolated spot, well away from most of the activity of New Society but we must take precautions. Move quickly, bending low and let's have no loud talking. Remember, when we get down into the populated area, it's all unknown territory and we don't know how we'll be received. So be ready for anything.'

Ahead of them, the smudge on the horizon grew then solidified into the coastline of Benarbor. August Richter steered for a spot on the beach he knew well from his numerous clandestine visits. Within a few minutes, the bows of the craft were scraping the shelving, stony beach.

The trio of invaders leaped out and, following a briefing given by Richter, they set about hauling the boat ashore on to dry land and turning it about, clear of the lapping waves.

They moved speedily, keeping closely together while Richter took the lead, guiding them through the barrier of rocks into the wildly overgrown portion of the interior. They trudged onward, broke cover close to the old Nissen hut and followed Richter through the doorless entrance into the musty interior.

Richter went at once to the pile of old boxes in the corner, rummaged among them and produced a large board fitted with switches and trailing wires. He held it up before his two companions.

'This is what I worked on over several trips to the island,' he said. 'It's the control panel allowing interference with the great man-made brain. It might look primitive but it has the potential to play havoc with the central element, the very nerve centre of the brain and throw the whole of the island into a state of chaos. All done by remote control. Now follow me down to the little building half hidden in the shrubbery and we'll ruin the reputation of the odious professor by bringing disaster on the great futuristic society he worked so hard to create. It will be a pleasure to know we made his name mud in the scientific community — before we get down to our real business with him!'

'And I can't wait for that,' said Stovic with a grim expression. He was a dogged and courageous fighter, a man well chosen by Richter.

'Nor can I,' declared Piankowski. 'You have stunning ability, Dr Richter, creating your equipment out of whatever components you could assemble and working in secret here, under the very noses of the professor and his friends.'

Richter gave a short, humourless laugh. 'Knowing he's working towards a just end can bring out the genius in a man,' he stated.

Richter's two colleagues followed him closely as, carrying the control panel under his arm, he made quick progress a short distance through the shrubbery, weeds and wild grass to the small out-station. In the gloomy interior, Piankowski and Stovic stared at the lined-up servos. The two had never seen such devices before and, to them they looked vaguely like a military squad though, individually, they did not resemble human beings.

'They're robots, the domestic servants of the New Society people,' said Richter. 'We designed such things in the early days of cybernetic studies before the war but never had a chance to create them. I believe somebody stored this group here then forgot about them. I was here a few times and adapted some of them to go into action when I do my stuff with the brain. When I give the signal, run out of here quickly and make for the back of this station. The adapted servos will come to life with their arms flailing dangerously. They'll roll out following a pre-coded route and go down the hill outside to make a nuisance of themselves in New Society. At the same time, there'll be wholesale disruption of every brain controlled device on the island.'

Richter bent down close to the long

metal conduit at the base of the bank of electrical controls. He laid his remote control panel on the ground, took two wires whose ends had been stripped of insulation. He inserted the bare wires firmly into the drilled holes in the conduit.

'*Now — run for it!*' he commanded urgently. Stovic and Piankowski ran for the door.

'*Get behind the building, well away from the entrance!*' shouted Richter. He threw a couple of switches on the control panel, stood up then went haring after his companions, hearing a humming rumble from the servos growing at his back.

12

Reckoning

Alec McLeith, part owner of Fort Airways, brought the Westland Lysander over the isle of Benarbor in the serene flying weather of a pleasant spring and began to lose altitude. He saw the imperfect surface of the landing strip below him and was puzzled by the fact that there was no sign of the usual squad of handlers who were on hand for a landing and who would help unload the cargo of supplies he was bringing in from the mainland

Furthermore, the van that usually waited close to the strip ready to convey the regular delivery of foodstuffs into New Society proper was not there.

Alec realised he would have to make a wholly solo landing and the lack of human life made him wonder if, for some reason, everyone had left the island. He brought the aircraft down to run bumpily over the old poorly repaired tarmac and slowed it to a halt.

McLeith shut off the engine, quit the aircraft and stood on the tarmac. He looked around in bewilderment. Then his ears caught the sound of a commotion going on some distance away where the airstrip ended, giving way to the tangles of stunted trees and untamed shrubbery which dominated this undeveloped portion of the island with its abandoned relics of wartime occupation.

He ran towards the sound of harsh voices and saw in a declivity in the land just where the tarmac ended, three dungaree clad figures fighting a grotesquely designed object which was mounted on a form of wheeled undercarriage. It had a sturdily built central body from which a set of arms protruded. The arms were whirling around and the object was fighting the men who were attempting to grab the arms and immobilise the object's action. While it was clearly a mechanical creation, it reacted to the interference as if it was a wild creature, seeming to have sentient consciousness and it gave off an angry buzzing like a savage growling.

On the ground close by, a similar device lay on its side with its wheels spinning and its arms twitching while making a similar, growling buzz. Two more men in dungarees sat on the ground, holding their heads, seeming to be half dazed. It was obvious to McLeith that this pair had fought the device, managing to conquer it by tipping it off its wheels but they had sustained severe blows from the milling arms.

McLeith came closer to the drama just as the two battling men managed to overcome the creature and send it crashing to the ground where, like its counterpart, it lay with wheels spinning while its multiple arms twitched and jerked ineffectively.

He rushed over to the men on the ground and helped each to his feet. One had suffered a crack on the head that made him wobble groggily and the second had received a severe blow to an eye. Though he was familiar with the servos as general helpers in New Society's house-holds, he never knew that they could function in the open air or that they could act aggressively. Furthermore, this pair seemed to have been adapted in some way and, for one thing, had more arms than most of their kind.

He was joined by the two men who had just grounded the second servo, gasping after their exertion. The four were the usual crew who helped out on the airstrip when he made his regular landings and take-offs.

'What on earth happened here?' he asked.

'Don't ask us,' breathed one. 'We were just getting ready for your arrival when this pair suddenly turned up. They seemed to come out of the bushes yonder and they obviously wanted to get on to the airstrip. You'll hardly credit it but they seemed to be intelligent. They gave us a hell of a fight with their arms thumping away at top speed. Fred was knocked on the head and Duncan was clouted in the eye.'

'Aye,' put in Duncan, 'but when I fell down, I just managed to grab that undercarriage arrangement they run on and tip the thing over.'

At the further end of the tarmac, a van came bouncing over the rough ground and halted on the landing strip. Only the developed roads of the New Society colony were equipped with the 'cat's eye' system by which Auntie controlled cars. In other parts of the island, vehicles had to contend with unpaved and rutted ground. The van regularly attended the airstrip when McLeith brought in supplies and was usually waiting when the Lysander touched down. On this occasion, it arrived late and its driver braked then left the vehicle to stride over to the men on the tarmac. He eyed the fallen servos with their still twitching arms and whirring wheels and gasped.

Hailing the five men, he called incredulously: 'Don't tell me it's happening up here, too! Down in New Society, there's total chaos. Some people have been driven out of their homes because their servos have gone haywire, running loose and attacking whoever is in the room. Some servos have somehow got out

177

into the streets and they're charging around endangering everyone. I was told all the functions powered by Auntie — the telephone system and all the electronically delivery systems to the shops and the restaurant and the cat's eyes in the roads — have failed, just as if Auntie had died. I was delayed by a pack of servos almost blocking the road with their arms spinning like windmills and bashing my van.' He nodded to McLeith's grounded Lysander. 'I can't see much point in unloading your plane, Alec. I wouldn't be able to deliver any stock, There's a war going on back yonder with some people trying to fight wild servos, others panicking and others taking shelter. Nobody seems to be able to restore order. New Society is so wonderful it has everything — except a police force!'

'Seems to me we should give a helping hand,' said McLeith.

He called to the overall clad airstrip hands: 'There's no point in standing about here, doing nothing. Are you men willing to go and see what can be done against the servos?'

'Aye, why not?' declared Duncan, who had been hit in the eye. 'I'd like to tip a few more of them off their wheels just to get even.' His three colleagues growled agreement.

'Are you willing to take us down into New Society, Hughie?' McLeith asked the van driver.

'Of course I am, but you can expect trouble from servos on the way,' said Hughie.

Alec McLeith took the seat next to the driver while the airstrip squad scrambled into the back of the empty van and the vehicle set off down the rough track that had served as a primitive road in the days when the island was used by the military. A quarter of a mile into the journey, they came upon a trio of servos which, in an uncanny way, appeared to be guarding the road.

As the van approached them, the servos, with their newly acquired facility for behaving in a totally unnatural manner since being unattached from their link to Auntie, started to whirl their arms and homed in on the vehicle.

179

At the wheel, Hughie put his foot down hard to increase speed and took the van bouncing recklessly over the ruts, running a brief gauntlet as servos thumped its sides with their spinning arms. The vehicle broke through on to clearer track and went onward to the more built up quarter of New Society proper. There, dotted about between the buildings they found pockets of sporadic action against servos in progress with some of the younger men grappling with the devices with their bare hands. Some of the defenders had learned the technique of knocking the servos off their wheels and, like wounded creatures, the fallen ones lay on the ground with their arms quivering and their wheels revolving. Groups of frightened people made a jittery audience looking as if they were ready to take to their heels at any second.

Hughie halted the van close to where three men were struggling to grasp the swinging arms of a servo which seemed to have an almost human tenacity. Alec McLeith, Hughie and the men from the airstrip leaped out of the van and immediately joined in the action. Alec stooped low, grasped the base of the servo and tipped the servo over.

One of the men who had been fighting it said breathlessly: 'Thanks. The damned thing nearly had us licked. Watch out for the buildings around here. Servos have been coming out of them if doors have been left open. Beats me how they can travel around when not plugged into Auntie but this whole place is crazy this morning.'

'I should say so,' panted one of his companions who was fighting for his breath after the tussle with the defiant servo. 'And it's because Auntie has gone completely crazy. The great notion of a society run by a giant brain is totally illogical. I don't know why I got involved in it in the first place. When you think of it it's nothing but a fancy form of dictatorship. After this affair, I'm packing up and leaving. I'd sooner have the old-fashioned life.'

While disruption raged in the nucleus of New Society, August Richter, closely followed by Piankowski and Stovic, led the way through the wind-stunted trees

181

and thick undergrowth of the undeveloped fringe of the settlement. The layout of the island was unknown to them but, as they traversed a ragged ridge, they eventually saw below them a clutter of roofs that marked the position of the housing section. They began to descend the ridge, heading towards the signs of civilisation. As they went, Richter removed the Luger from an inner pocket of his work-stained sports jacket and transferred it to a handier outer pocket.

At precisely the same time, Hereward Hynes pushed his way out of a knot of angry people at the door of the restaurant. Like them he had just heard an announcement from the manager that breakfast could not be served because the delivery of cooked food, delivered electronically, courtesy of Auntie, had not materialised. Hynes saw no point in bad-tempered demonstrations. He knew there was wholesale chaos in New Society and it was obvious that all the services dependent on Auntie were in a state of collapse.

On his way to the restaurant he saw a couple of prowling servos which although lacking any features that gave them the appearance of creatures of flesh and blood, seemed to be on the lookout for prey. Still feeling stiff and aching after the fight with the servos a couple of nights before, he gave them a wide berth and reached the restaurant by a circuitous route.

He was aware of sounds of commotion from nearby as he left the restaurant and supposed a battle with rogue servos was in progress. The clash between Ted Clemence, himself and the servos two nights before had left him with a suspicion of the robotic devices bordering on the superstitious and he had unplugged his own servo's lead from the point in the wall and laid the device on the floor, rendering its wheels ineffective.

In the midst of the bewildered group who were denied breakfast at the restaurant, he heard complaints of their servos starting up of their own accord, in some cases menacing their owners and, in others, escaping through open doors with their arms spinning dangerously. Something like the disaster foretold in the warning notes sent to Sir Elkanah Artingstall seemed to have descended on New Society.

Hynes wondered what could be done to restore order and his thoughts turned to Archnov and his group of academic cronies, though they had proved of little use in coming to grips with Auntie's earlier aberrations. He headed for New Society's administrative building where they were most likely to be found. On the way, he met Ted Clemence who was heading for the restaurant.

'If you're hoping for breakfast, Ted, you've had it,' he called, falling back into using the popular slang of the forces in the recent war.

'That's what I thought. I've been making my way here, dodging servos. The blasted things are wheeling around looking for trouble,' answered Clemence. 'I guessed the restaurant would be affected by the revolt just like everywhere else but thought I'd look in and size up the situation. I suppose you know all the telephones are out of action, all the electric lighting, too. It's exactly what I expected to happen — the complete collapse of a society.'

Clemence decided to join Hynes in the

search for Archnov and the professors. They were found huddled in the entrance to the administration building as if sheltering from a storm: Archnov, Jones, Estcourt, Thorne and Glassman against whose name in Hynes' mental card-index system there was now a large question mark. Did the scholarly academic who prowled at night near the isolated outstation have a hand in creating the present chaotic situation in New Society? Was he playing some deep game of sabotage?

Archnov looked both startled and bewildered by the manner in which the technological and social experiment he had largely planned and nurtured was disintegrating before his eyes. Hynes and Clemence approached him and asked if they could be of any use in quelling the disorder.

Archnov, looking dazed, said he did not know if anything could be done. Most of Auntie's functions had clearly shut down but a portion of the brain, governing the actions of the servos was still working in a highly erratic and ungovernable manner.

Just as Hynes and Clemence encountered the professors at the administration building, three gaunt, roughly garbed men came out of the fringe of untamed land and set foot in New Society proper. Here and there were groups of people and several grounded servos, casualties of recent battles but while there was no belligerent action in progress, there was tension and bewilderment in the air.

August Richter, leader of the trio, stopped a man and questioned him.

'Do you know where we can find the man you call Archnov?' he asked.

The man was one of the angry ones who expressed strong feelings about New Society at the recent meeting. The heavy Germanic accent of this grim, craggy faced stranger plainly intrigued him and he answered: 'No. I don't know why you want him but if I spot him I'll black both his eyes. He and his boffin chums built up this place with wonderful promises and now it's falling down around us.' He jerked his thumb, indicating some buildings behind him and added: 'If it's any use to you, he and his cronies are usually somewhere around the administration building and that's over yonder.'

Richter grunted his thanks and he, Stovic and Piankowski hurried off in the direction indicated, leaving a cluster of New Society people wondering about the coarse-looking obvious foreigners who had arrived in their midst as if dropped from the sky.

At the entrance to the administration building, Hynes noted the mood of the people who were demanding answers. He recalled the strain of anger displayed at the meeting where Archnov and his colleagues admitted they were at a loss to explain why Auntie had set off on her course of erratic behaviour. Now, the anger was much more pronounced, growing stronger and decidedly menacing.

'Don't you think you'd be better off inside the building?' he asked the group of boffins. 'You'd think more calmly in a more peaceful atmosphere.'

'We can't open the doors,' said Estcourt, who was displaying signs of acute jitters. 'Auntie locks all the doors nightly as a matter of security and every one is firmly fastened, otherwise, we'd be inside. These people are anything but friendly.'

'He's right,' muttered Ted Clemence. 'Any minute now, they'll be baying for blood.'

The gathering in front of the building was becoming a crowd. As in any crisis, news spread quickly and word of where Archnov and his chief men could be found went the rounds speedily. The leading boffins were seen as the authors of all the ills that had descended on New Society and were now in the position of many leaders of revolutions. After a time, they fell out of popular favour.

Hynes saw that Archnov, now looking thoroughly scared, and his colleagues were in no position to make an appeal to reason and, if they were they would be scorned. He decided to try taking some venom out of the situation and, standing on the top step of the short flight in front of the building, raised a hand.

'Ladies and gentlemen, please be calm,' he called. 'There's no point in losing your tempers. I know everything has gone wrong but the only sensible thing we can do is to keep cool and co-operate to put things on a workable basis.'

A woman began to heckle. 'It's all very well for you to talk, Mr Herford. You're just an outsider who came here to write a book. Well, you've got your story and it's not the wonderful success tale the university would like you to tell. It's all disillusion and betrayal. We've staked our careers and futures on New Society and it's turned out to be a vast fraud.'

'The lady's right, Herford,' yelled a man. 'Archnov and his crew led us up the garden path. And look at them now — they don't know which way to turn. After this fiasco, they should be punished.'

Grunts of approval rumbled through the crowd, suggesting that there was an appetite for violent retribution.

Then, three figures pushed their way through the crowding bodies and their appearance caused the disconcerted growling to die. They were led by a thin, rugged man who carried a black Luger, levelled at the ready and they strode directly for the entrance of the administration building. Hynes took in their rough working clothes, some of it made up of elements of old military garb and their distinctly Slavic faces. The sight of the trio coupled with a fact concerning Archnov which he secretly possessed equated to a total understanding of what they were and their purpose.

As his brain absorbed the meaning of this intrusion, he heard the man with the Luger bark harshly: 'Viktor Pyotrich, calling yourself Professor Leonid Archnov, Commandant Viktor Pyotrich, we have come for you! Pyotrich, murderer and war criminal, do you remember me — August Richter; of Vienna University, and a victim of your thievery? Commandant Pyotrich, you are about to be made to answer for your past!'

On the upper step, Archnov, now unmasked as a man with a totally different identity, stood as though frozen with his mouth open. His face was white, causing the birthmark on his forehead to appear even redder than usual. He stared at the man with the pistol as if he was a vision from the realm of malignant ghosts.

Then, as though shot from a gun, he darted down the steps at top speed and

190

plunged into the crowd at the base of the steps. He began to push and elbow his way through it in panicky desperation. The man with the pistol spat out an expletive as he and his companions whirled around just in time to see Pyotrich lose himself in the mass of bodies.

To shoot now would mean hitting some innocent person. With Hynes and Clemence joining them, they gave chase and, pushing and shoving, they tried to get a clear run through the crowd.

The crowd began to thin out in reaction to the knowledge that a man with a firearm was in their midst. Pyotrich was approaching its far fringe when a man tried to grab him and received a severe punch in the face.

The fleeing man and his pursuers broke clear of the crowd and Pyotrich began to lose ground. Hynes' long legs took him a few paces ahead of the others.

'Give yourself up!' he managed to yell in spite of his panting. 'We know you were an SS man!'

Pyotrich took no heed and ran on blindly, so blindly that he tripped over one of the devices of the new Utopia he had such a leading role in fashioning — a fallen servo, pushed off its wheels in the earlier disturbances.

He picked himself up, looked around wildly and, fighting for his breath, tried to resume his running but Hynes lurched forward and grabbed his jacket. He hauled Pyotrich toward him, grasped his lapels and began to shake him vigorously as if he were a rag doll.

He placed his face close to Pyotrich's sweating visage. 'Can't you see you're finished?' he breathed. 'I know your true background and what you did in the war will all come out and you will never run away from it. Take your chance in court!'

Pyotrich snarled and wriggled with undiminished energy and suddenly drove a knee forcefully into Hynes' stomach.

Hynes' breath gusted out of him and he felt an excruciating pain in his intestines. He doubled up, losing his grip on Pyotrich's coat. Pyotrich reeled backward, seeing, as if it was the stuff of nightmares, a vision of vengeful faces closing in on him relentlessly. The lean man, wielding his menacing Luger, was to the fore of them.

In the close vicinity, he saw a face he knew — that of Alec McLeith, the young pilot from the mainland. He and the men from the airstrip had been attracted to the activities in front of the administration building and had followed subsequent developments to reach this point. Pyotrich sped towards him. Before he knew what was happening, McLeith was clutched by Pyotrich who was wholly possessed by fevered panic. He hauled the aviator towards himself, whirled the young man around and placed himself behind him. He flung an arm around his neck and held it tightly in the crook of his elbow. He pushed his free hand into the front of his jacket and, from an inner pocket, brought out a small automatic pistol.

It was plain that he intended to hold McLeith as a hostage with the gun at his head. Hynes, Clemence and the three displaced persons fanned out in front of him, frozen into inaction.

Unheeding of their distance from the airstrip, in a gasping, jittery voice, Pyotrich said: 'Get me to your plane and fly me out of here — to anywhere!'

In a half-throttled voice, Alec McLeith answered: 'Can't — there's not enough fuel!'

'You're too far from the airstrip and he'll only have enough fuel to reach the mainland. That'll do you no good. You'll easily be caught by the police,' called Ted Clemence, the veteran RAF pilot. 'Give yourself up, you damned fool!'

There was a second drama beginning to unfold before the eyes of the spectators but it was unseen by Pyotrich because it was going on behind his back. Just as Pyotrich produced the automatic pistol from his inner pocket, a figure detached itself from a knot of watchers close to his rear and moved swiftly with cat-like stealth and silence behind him.

Pyotrich did not hold the weapon to McLeith's head but flourished it in an almost triumphant demonstration to let the watchers know he possessed it. This gave the man behind him his momentary chance. He pounced, grabbed the hand holding the gun and yanked Pyotrich backwards, causing him to fire harmlessly into the air, at the same time releasing his grip on McLeith's neck.

As he fell flat on his back, Pyotrich dropped his gun and the watching group came to life, rushing forward to lay hands on him. Hereward Hynes, though still winded from the blow in the stomach, struggled to force himself into the rush. He reached Pyotrich, grasped him and helped others to pull him to his feet.

Throughout all this last frantic action, Hynes behaved almost mechanically, like a man hypnotised or one in a dream, scarcely believing what he had witnessed a few seconds before.

For the man who attacked Pyotrich from the rear, overpowered him and brought him to the ground with the speed of forked lightning was the calm, scholarly, straggly moustached prowler of the night, Dr Glassman.

13

Explanations

'Yes, I admit it was a calculated risk,' said Dr Glassman. 'My heart was in my mouth as I took it. I was sure Pyotrich would place that gun to McLeith's head as a threat and knew I had hardly a second in which to act before he brought it any closer. Mercifully, I moved at just the right moment. Looking back, I shudder to think how easily McLeith might have been hit when the gun went off. A close shave, but I've taken calculated risks before and, so far, always come off best.'

Glassman was part of a tight group of men occupying the front steps of the administration building, some standing and others sitting. In the middle, seated on a step and carefully guarded by Piankowski and Stovic, who were clearly in no mood to be trifled with, was Viktor

Pyotrich, so recently known to so many present as Professor Leonid Archnov. With a permanent scowl, he now looked totally deflated. There was about him no trace of the schoolboy slang quoting and assumed hearty, 'more-British-than-the British' persona.

The company on the step included Hereward Hynes, Ted Clemence, the aircraft handlers from the landing strip and the group of boffins who had once surrounded the leader they knew as Professor Archnov. Missing was Dr August Richter whom Hughie, the van driver had driven up to the outstation in the untamed country near the loch. He was on a mission to reactivate his makeshift remote control equipment in the outstation with which he tapped into the very core of Auntie's electronic workings.

Just as he had thrown out of kilter her control of myriad functions, including governance of the squads of servos, he claimed that, from that control point, he could reverse the mischief he had created by stirring Auntie into life and setting her off on her old orderly path of behaviour. Thus the telephone service should restart, the opening of securely locked doors and much more should also be accomplished.

Alec McLeith was also missing. Because the telephones were dead, he, too, had travelled in Hughie's van to the landing strip to fly his Lysander to Fort Calaige to inform the police that officers were required on Benarbor, preferably with a representative of Special Branch among them, and to request that they flew back with him.

Now and again, the people of New Society, who had invested the bulk of the men on the steps with a form of authority, came to ask when things would be back to something like normal. Patience was counselled and they were told that Auntie would very soon be back in action.

Hynes and Clemence were standing with Dr Glassman and Glassman's comment about his calculated risks brought a twinkle of humour to Hynes' eye.

'Don't you find that risks can sometimes blow back on one, particularly if one takes them in wild places in the thick of bushes and tangled undergrowth on dark nights, Dr Glassman?' he asked with an expression of absolute innocence.

Glassman fingered the bruise on his face. With a twinkle in his eye matching that in Hynes' he said: 'Ah, you mean the dangers of walking into the edge of a door?'

'Yes, a door shaped rather like myself.'

'Sorry about that. You really do deserve an explanation. You see, on the very same night right after you and Mr Clemence were attacked by aggressive servos and went to see our scowling friend here about it, he called a meeting of us boffins. Although it was late, he proposed that we scout around to see if there had been any other incidents and note the locations where they happened. Knowledge of a location might give a clue to where a specific portion of the brain needed attention.

'I was detailed to take a look at that remote region where you two were attacked and I recalled the presence of that almost lost outstation. I had a vague notion that some servos were stored there and were, likewise, almost lost. It seemed a promising area to investigate. For days,

I had been thinking that, if there really was a mysterious saboteur either among the community on the island or somehow making visits from outside, he must be tapping into Auntie's very bloodstream so to speak. It seemed that this almost neglected outstation, so close to the shoreline could easily be his base of operations.'

'I see, and you blundered into me and thought you'd found the intruder,' commented Hynes.

'Yes, at first, But after I hit you and you went down, I learned I was wrong,' said Glassman. 'You were probably too dazed to remember but there was a very thin moon coming and going that night. When you were down, it came out of the clouds briefly and showed your face. I knew Hereward Hynes was on the up and up and not the saboteur and I didn't want to face any complications following the incident. I had another, far more important matter to deal with so I made a quick retreat. I hoped you hadn't recognised me but you did give me a big enough distinguishing mark when you thumped me. I do apologise for the rough stuff, Mr Hynes.'

'Did you say 'Hynes', Dr Glassman?' asked a bewildered Ted Clemence who was standing next to Hynes and had heard Glassman's narrative. 'Do you mean Hynes, the detective who was in the papers a few weeks ago — for breaking up a black market gang, as I remember it?'

The answer came from Hynes himself. Grinning, he said; 'The very same, Ted. I'm sorry to have deceived you. I was acting for the university and it was thought I should become Edgar Herford, a supposed writer. And rounding up a gang of black market spivs was a lot less tangled than this present affair.'

Hughie's van drove up, halted in front of the group on the steps and disgorged Dr August Richter with a triumphant expression on his lean face.

'I've fixed everything,' he called, 'Auntie is back in action and should behave normally. Try the doors. They should be unlocked and the telephones and everything else should be working.'

After making this delivery, Hughie left, saying he had to return to the airstrip to await the return of Alec McLeith.

Someone tested the doors of the reception area of the administration building and swung them open. With sighs of relief, the whole company on the steps trooped into the hall with Pyotrich pushed along by Piankowski and Stovic in a hardly gentle manner.

When the group had settled into the new location, the telephones were tested, found to be working and Hynes contacted the police headquarters in Fort Calaige. He reported back that Alec McLeith had already arrived there and was even then at the station, preparing to fly back with a couple of detective officers.

Richter felt the whole of New Society deserved an explanation of all the recent disruptions and he told the group how he and his fellow DPs set out to ruin the man known as Archnov, working from the boatyard within reach of Benarbor.

'We were alerted to his work on the island through an article on it in a magazine after a group of us, all previously in Trolinka, a camp of slave labourers in Ukraine, were brought to Scotland. We knew his real identity from a published photograph. The man in the photo was described as Feodor Archnov but his facial birthmark gave him away. He was Viktor Pyotrich, one of the worst of the Nazi guards at Trolinka.

'Pyotrich was a Ukrainian who collaborated with the Nazi invaders and was recruited into the Waffen SS, made up of those willing to join the Nazis after their countries were subjugated. I knew him from an earlier date, as a student of electronics and cybernetics at the University of Kiev. During that nightmare time, the summer of 1939, when Stalin and Hitler were short-lived partners through the Berlin-Moscow agreement, he was one of a visiting party from Kiev who came to the University of Vienna, where I was a faculty member, working in the same disciplines.'

Richter paused and glowered across at the captive Pyotrich, standing between his stolid guards, Stovic and Piankowski. Pyotrich glowered back.

'You'd hardly think it to see him now,' said Richter, 'but he was quite a personable young man; a bit of an actor and a wag. We became friends but I later found he stole some of my most valuable research papers and took them back to Kiev. Later, in 1943, as a Waffen SS guard at Trolinka, Pyotrich played a bloody part in putting down a revolt by the slave labourers. Machine guns were used mercilessly and Pyotrich killed with enjoyment. After that, he was rewarded with promotion out of the Waffen SS of conquered enemies to full member of the SS proper. Then he was made commandant of a concentration camp in Poland, a stepping stone to the gas chambers of the extermination camps.'

'And I know plenty about that,' commented another voice — surprisingly, that of Dr Glassman. All eyes turned to him but he simply stood, calm-faced and scholarly as usual, showing no inclination to explain himself.

Richter went on: 'From what I know of your brain here on Benarbor, so largely designed by the supposed Archnov, he incorporated knowledge pioneered by myself in it. That helped me to tap into it and wreak havoc with its functions. It was all intended to pull the professor's work apart to disgrace him before we sailed in and exposed him. I regret some of the incidents I heard of like the servo attacks on the baby and others and the mishap with the car on the road, all part of my fumbling by remote control but it seems no real harm was done.'

'And what do you know of those peculiar letters sent to Sir Elkanah, warning of disaster coming to New Society?' asked Hynes.

'The work of a zealot among our people but done without my knowledge,' said Richter. 'You must understand that men who have endured years in our wretched situation sometimes develop eccentric notions — though, on reflection, I'm not sure this gentleman's notions are all that eccentric. He was merely opposed to life dominated by a great brain and was quite harmless and totally without malice. He thought Sir Elkanah should devote funds to other purposes.'

Richter was approached by Dr Glassman. 'Dr Richter, as one electronics man to another, may I say you deserve a Nobel Prize for your work on cybernetics?' he said. 'Stopping and starting Auntie the way you did was magnificent, especially when you had to work with home-made equipment and all speedily made in your secret visits to the island.'

Hereward Hynes faced Glassman. 'How about some explaining from you, Dr Glassman?' he said. 'Why were you so determined to disarm Pyotrich, even in such a hazardous way with what you called a calculated risk? And you said you've taken calculated risks before. I believe you. There's more to you than meets the eye. What is it?'

'Oh, my dear Mr Hynes, I'm a very simple soul, just a scholarly scientist but I might lift the veil of mystery a little if you tell all of us how you knew Pyotrich had been in the SS. It was a carefully concealed fact but you shouted that you knew it as we chased him.'

Hynes acquiesced. 'Very well,' he said. 'But Mr Clemence, here and Miss Tilly Budd have a part in the story.'

'Me?' gasped a wide-eyed Ted Clemence.

'What have I got to do with it? And who's Miss Tilly Budd?'

'Miss Tilly Budd is my secretary in London who, with excellent efficiency, supplied me with a wealth of ammunition. It was valuable information concerning the claims of the rather deflated gentleman yonder whom we used to call Archnov. You might recall relating the account of his wartime life as he gave it to his staff in the earlier days of New Society. You might have cut some corners but I'm sure you gave it accurately.'

Clemence looked at him in a puzzled fashion. 'I'm sure I did, so far as I remember,' he said.

'And part of his tale was that, after the collapse of his Ukrainian unit in the fight against the German invaders, he was on the run and made his way to Odessa, then under Nazi occupation. From there, he managed to take a neutral tramp steamer to Turkey, on the other side of the Black Sea. But that was the giveaway portion of his tale. At that period, the Soviet navy on the Black Sea was reeling from Hitler's surprise attack on Russia. In the Odessa region, it came under devastating attacks from the Nazi air force and the navies of the Nazis' allies, Bulgaria and Rumania and even German and Italian ships that had managed to reach that distant location. With heavy losses, the Russian ships had to evacuate and relocate far away on the Georgian side of the sea. The Black Sea was a furious scene of sea battles, submarine attacks, air raids and mine-laying. You can bet no neutral tramp steamer dared to sail those waters where there was absolutely no place for neutrality.'

Hynes glanced across at Pyotrich. 'You slipped up there, didn't you, Professor?' he called. 'But you were not stupid. Stupidity was never part of the SS tradition, was it?'

'Go to hell!' spat Pyotrich.

'Ah, but your account of your next leg of the journey was thought out much more convincingly,' continued Hynes. 'Your story was that, from Turkey, you flew to Britain with some of the Turkish air cadets due to be trained by the RAF. Full marks for knowledge of minor points of the history of the war, Pyotrich, for such cadets were trained here until Turkey decided to stay neutral and not join the Allies. It gave an authentic touch to your presentation of yourself as a gallant Ukrainian fleeing his conquered homeland to reach Britain and continue fighting.

'In reality, you joined the Waffen SS with others who abandoned their countrymen and Dr Richter has told us of your villainous career. My guess is that you were another war criminal who gave the Allies the slip at the end of the war and somehow got yourself into the stream of refugees admitted to Britain when, as is now admitted, checks on identity were lax. You invented an impressive tale of working for the British war effort and bamboozled your way into the university world. Your skills and knowledge are sound and you eventually were given a professorial chair and put in charge of a grand scheme of building a great dream society with an electronic brain at its core.'

Ted Clemence was looking at Hynes with mingled incredulity and admiration. 'How did you gather all that information?' he asked.

'Ah, the donkey work was done by the admirable Miss Tilly Budd in London,' answered Hynes. 'I was suspicious about the story of the neutral tramp steamer though I had only a vague knowledge of the war on that front. I phoned Miss Budd and asked her to do a detailed check on aspects of the history of the war in my fairly extensive library, make notes and phone me back. Miss Budd is an absolute gem, although she hates to be told so.'

'But how did you know Archnov, as we called him, was in the SS?' asked Clemence.

'You were with me the night I made that discovery, though I kept quiet about it,' Hynes said. 'Remember how we called on him the night the servos attacked us and he answered the door stripped to the waist? You might not recall it but he threw a towel over his right shoulder. It was all done very quickly but I just happened to catch a glimpse of the clue to why he did it.

'He wanted to cover a line of tattoo letters and figures on his upper arm. Those indicated his blood group. It was a trick of the Nazis to guard their treasured SS from ever being given a transfusion of blood that was not 'Aryan' or Jewish should they be seriously wounded. And they showed they must really have treasured Archnov by tattooing him for he's not what the Nazis called 'Aryan' but a Slav, a people they despised.'

Ted Clemence gave an ironic laugh and declared: 'Which all goes to show the fatuous racial theories of the Nazis. Modern anthropology has exploded the notion of any connection between race and blood. One can no more have English blood than French, Dutch or American blood. And since the Jews are not a race but a religious grouping, one cannot have Jewish blood any more than Catholic, Protestant or Muslim blood.'

'I think,' said the modest voice of Dr Glassman, 'I should take this opportunity to admit to Mr Hynes' observation that there is more to myself than meets the eye.'

From an inside pocket, he produced a small printed card which he passed to Hynes whose eyes widened as he read it.

He passed it to Clemence.

Clemence looked at it, saw a row of characters which he immediately recognised as Hebrew then the words: '*The Abrahamic League*' under which there was further Hebrew text and a signature: '*Saul Glassman.*'

'The Abrahamic League,' said Hynes. 'You're the people who go into some rare corners of the world, tracking down fugitive Nazi war criminals. You started right after the war and you pulled in some prize catches. You recently collected a bunch in South America. You've been known to hunt mercilessly for them and bring them to justice. You skip over international boundaries and tangle with politicians, judges, magistrates and police who're reluctant to release whoever you want. It's fair to say you're not above what some might call 'kidnapping'. I remember you said you've taken some calculated risks.'

'I'm admitting nothing,' smiled Glassman. 'I'm just a simple university lecturer. Admittedly, I angled for my present post chiefly to watch Archnov, as he called himself. The League has a dossier on him. He would be dealt with in due course but the activities of the DPs on the mainland were totally unknown until Dr Richter and his friends turned up here. No matter, our professor will face properly organised justice.'

The doors of the administration centre swung open and newly landed Alec McLeith entered, flanked by two solidly built men in raincoats and trilby hats, the 'uniform' of the ununiformed detective police. The heavier of the two, a man of commanding presence, announced: 'I'm Detective Chief Superintendent Donaldson and this is Detective Chief Inspector Drake. We've been in touch with high authorities in London and find there are several international warrants out for the man known as Archnov. We'll caution him and hold him. Other officers are coming by boat to take him into custody.'

He produced a notebook and a fountain pen from his coat pocket, and laid them on the entrance hall's desk. 'A few statements must be taken but I'm sure you will have much to do at the moment. All of you please write your names in the book and reassemble here in an hour and a half from now when our other officers will be present.'

Piankowski and Stovic remained with the two policemen to guard Pyotrich and the group in the entrance hall broke off to attend to various aspects of bringing a semblance of normal life back to New Society.

Dr Glassman was off in one corner deep in conversation with August Richter. 'Whichever way our experiment here goes after all these developments, I'm sure the University of Central UK will keep it going,' he said. 'There'll be many opportunities for research and one with your knowledge and skills would be more than an asset. I'm confident my fellow boffins will join me in urging Chancellor Artingstall to recommend that you become a colleague in our work.'

As Hereward Hynes and Ted Clemence walked down the steps of the administration building, Hynes stopped for a moment and squinted off into the distance where he could see the white dome of Auntie's nerve centre making a pleasant picture on its hill, brightened by the strong sunshine. He chuckled and said: 'Just for a moment, Ted, I thought Auntie was smiling at us. Perhaps she was offering us her congratulations.'

THE COMIC BOOK KILLER

Richard A. Lupoff

Hobart Lindsey is a quiet man, a bachelor living with his widowed mother in the suburbs and working as an insurance claims agent. Marvia Plum is a tough, savvy, street-smart cop. Then fate throws the unlikely pair together. A burglary at a vintage comic book store leads to a huge insurance claim that Lindsey must investigate for his company — and to the brutal murder of the store owner, for which Marvia must find the killer. Lindsey and Plum, like oil and water — but working together to unravel a baffling mystery!

THE GREEN PEN MYSTERY

Donald Stuart

Caught in a thunderstorm one hot summer night, Peter Lake takes shelter in a public call-box. When the telephone begins to ring, and curiosity prompts him to answer, a desperate plea for help issues from the receiver — then a scream — then silence. His determination to assist the owner of the mystery voice will fling him headlong into uncharted seas of crime, danger and sudden death . . . Meanwhile, Adam Kane, brilliant and unorthodox solicitor, brings his powerful intellect to bear on four baffling cases.